D0045829

RED, WHITE, AND BLUE MURDER

RED, WHITE, AND BLUE MURDER

A HILDA JOHANSSON MYSTERY

Jeanne M. Dams

Walker & Company ✺ New York

First published in the United States of America in 2000 by
Walker Publishing Company, Inc.

Published simultaneously in Canada by Fitzhenry and Whiteside,
Markham, Ontario L3R 4T8

Library of Congress Cataloging-in-Publication Data

Dams, Jeanne M.
  Red, white, and blue murder : a Hilda Johannson mystery/Jeanne M. Dams.
  p. cm.
  ISBN 0-8027-3341-7
  1. Studebaker family—Fiction. 2. Women domestics—Indiana
—South Bend—Fiction. 3. South Bend (Ind.)—Fiction. I. Title.
PS3554.A498 R44 2000
813'.54—dc21

                                                        00-022216

Series design by M. J. DiMassi

Printed in the United States of America
2 4 6 8 10 9 7 5 3 1

Preface

In this account of real historical events mixed with fictional ones, I have quoted freely from newspapers. I have sometimes, however, added a few words pertaining to the fictional side of the story. All quotations directly related to the health of President McKinley are verbatim.

I have arranged the weather to suit myself.

Life is well known for its habit of imitating art. I did not know, until I was well into the writing of this book, that the assassin Leon Czolgosz did in fact visit South Bend shortly before he shot President McKinley. What had seemed a useful fictional device suddenly became reality, to the considerable surprise of the author! I have no idea what he really did here, nor whom he met, since those who saw him were, as the South Bend *Tribune* said, "understandably reluctant to have their names in the newspaper." Therefore, the actions attributed to him within the pages of this book are, save for the assassination itself, entirely the product of my imagination. If something similar took place in real life, it is (I hope and trust) not my fault.

On the other hand, all actions and quotations attributed to Emma Goldman, one of America's most notable anarchists, are authentic. To my knowledge, she was never in South Bend.

I have tried to write with the attitudes that prevailed during the period in which the story takes place. Thus there are unflattering references to foreigners, immigrants, and the like, which are not meant to reflect my attitudes, nor those of the residents of today's South Bend who, every year, celebrate a massive Ethnic Festival, taking joyous note of the diversity of our city, especially its food!

I have not, in my research, met with any indication that the first Studebaker automobile trial was kept a secret. On the other hand, neither have I seen any extensive early publicity. So, with the freedom afforded the writer of fiction, I chose the option that made the better story. Another of my story lines, the hint of labor problems at the Studebaker factory, is made up out of whole cloth. The policies and attitudes of the Studebaker brothers kept their business remarkably free of labor conflicts (with one minor exception in 1893) until a much later period than the one with which I am concerned (a time, indeed, when all the brothers were dead and their principles no longer governed the company they had founded).

The real contractor for the new city hall (which really was built by James Oliver) was one H. G. Christman, whose firm is still esteemed in South Bend. There were, so far as I know, no untoward incidents during the construction of the building, and certainly no hint of scandal has ever accrued to Christman. City Hall, once completed, was a handsome Romanesque building that served South Bend well until it was, with utter disregard for its historical and architectural significance, torn down in the 1970s.

RED, WHITE, AND BLUE MURDER

1

Mrs. Clem Studebaker gave a luncheon at her home,
Tippecanoe place, Saturday afternoon. There were 27 la-
dies present and luncheon was served in the dining room.
The table decorations were beautiful. . . .
—South Bend *Tribune*, January 1, 1900, page 1

ILDA, that stifling August evening, was both rushed off
her feet and bored out of her mind.
"Talk, talk, talk," she grumbled to Norah as they whisked
back to the butler's pantry for dessert plates. "If they have
nothing to say, why do they not remain silent?"

"You're just grumpy. You always get grumpy when it's hot."
Norah sniffed and handed Hilda a stack of plates. "A fine sort of
dinner party that'd be, with all of 'em sittin' around sayin'
nothin'. Here, them are the Meissen—mind you don't drop
'em!"

It was a small party, as Tippecanoe Place parties went, easily
contained in the family dining room. Only eight couples shared
the table with Colonel and Mrs. George Studebaker, nearly all,
Hilda knew, connected by business ties with Studebaker Brothers manufacturing.

It would, in Hilda's opinion, have been much wiser for her
employers to work off their business obligations with a larger
party. Not that anyone would be interested in the opinions of
the housemaid. But she knew just as well as the Studebakers
that large dinners allowed for an interesting mix of guests at
each table. With only eighteen people sitting around a single

table, the possibility for devastating boredom was much greater.

The host and hostess were doing their best. Mrs. George had, with Mrs. Sullivan, the cook, planned an elaborate menu, much of it to be served chilled in deference to the sweltering August weather. She had also taken great care to seat her guests so as to separate those with any of the little animosities business can so easily generate. Now she and Colonel George were trying hard to keep the conversation going, but it was uphill work.

As Hilda set out the dessert plates, she amused herself by studying the guests. How surprised they would be if they realized how much the unregarded servants knew about them! Mrs. Avery, for example, a frequent guest seated to Colonel George's right, was a flirt and a social climber. Dressed, in her Paris gown and her diamonds, more for a ball than a simple dinner, she was by far the most attractive woman in the room. And she knew it, thought Hilda as she set the fragile plate in front of her. At twenty-five or so she was also by several years the youngest woman present, and seemed determined to conquer every man in the room. No matter what Colonel George or Mr. Coates, her other dinner partner, said to her, she batted her eyelashes and laughed. It was a very feminine, high, tinkly laugh, and Hilda was beginning to be very tired of it.

Her husband, Mr. Avery, a well-to-do lumber dealer and a much older man, might have been able to keep her quiet, but since the Averys were the principal guests, he was of course seated at the other end of the table, at his hostess's right hand. A pity husbands and wives couldn't sit together, for Mr. Avery knew how to behave at a dinner party. He smiled, he spoke courteously to his hostess and others near him, he was gallant with all the ladies, he even smiled at the servants. He kept up a light banter of conversation, insubstantial perhaps, but pleasant. Hilda knew that Mr. Avery liked money perhaps a little more than he should, but she approved of him.

Mr. Coates, the attorney seated next to Mrs. Avery, was no use at all. His manner was as dry as the legal documents he dealt with for the Studebakers. He spoke when spoken to, offered a comment or two on the weather, and asked for the salt to be passed. Most of the time he simply chewed his food. Hilda considered Norah's remark. Perhaps she was right, and no talk at all was even worse than silly talk.

Mrs. Harriman, next to Mr. Coates, was a worthy woman in a steel-gray gown and a steel-boned corset. The wife of another attorney, she sat on charity boards and hospital boards and chaired ladies' societies in aid of one thing and another. She did, in short, all the things Mrs. Avery ought to do if she really wanted to rise in the social scale. But Mrs. Avery was far too frivolous for such boring pursuits, and certainly she would never find them a topic for conversation. Mrs. Harriman talked about them all, discoursing on their achievements and the great needs still to be met, from the oysters, to the vichyssoise and the fish, right through to the jellied chicken and the salad. Perhaps, Hilda speculated, she talked to keep her mind off all the good food she dared not try to stuff into that rigidly corseted body.

Of Mr. Singler, the banker to Mrs. Harriman's right, Hilda knew little. The Singlers were new in town and had been to dinner only once before, a huge affair for which Hilda's duties had kept her away from the guests. (By rights the head housemaid, Hilda served at table only for the small parties, when outside help was not needed.) From his conversation she gathered that he was a passionate golfer; he could speak only of great courses he had played, of his own strengths and weaknesses, of new equipment he was eager to try.

All of which Mrs. Harriman steadfastly ignored, while Mrs. Warren, to his right, said such things as "Oh, really? Imagine that. Dear me, is that bad? Oh, good, I see!" and crumbled her dinner roll. She wore a gown Hilda had seen several times before. The pink silk clashed badly with her complexion, and the lace was looking slightly grubby. Hilda considered her to be a poor, mousy excuse for a woman. Of course Mr. Warren, a well-known contractor who had worked often for the Studebakers, was a bully. You had only to look at his wife to know that. But really, why couldn't the woman stick up for herself? If anybody tried to bully *her*, Hilda . . . well, he would be sorry!

The plates were all in place; Hilda and Norah retired to the background to let Anton, the footman, and Mr. Williams, the butler, serve the charlotte russe. While Hilda waited for her next chore, wishing she could sit down and rest her aching feet, she considered the rest of the party. About Mr. Slick, sitting next to Mrs. Warren, she knew only that he was an engraver who worked extensively with Studebaker's. He and his pretty wife seemed inoffensive enough people. By coincidence or design, Mrs. Slick was sitting next to Mr. Warren on the other side of the table, and did not appear to be enjoying herself very much. Mr. Warren wasn't bullying her, though. He was another of the silent ones, spending his time on his food and ignoring both Mrs. Slick and tall, willowy Mrs. Singler on his other side.

Hilda didn't know the woman next to Mr. Slick at all, but the last man on that side was a neighbor, Mr. Cushing, whom she knew very well indeed. He and his wife had obviously been invited to help the Studebakers with a rather sticky party; they were old friends who lived in the next block, next door to the house where Hilda's sister, Freya, worked as a maid. Mrs. George had cleverly seated both of them close to her, Mrs. Cushing being just next to Mr. Warren, to help keep conversation going. She would, thought Hilda, have done better to put one of them at the other end of the table, where Colonel George was having a hard time of it.

He could get nothing but titters out of Mrs. Avery, and Mrs. Singler, on his other side, simply agreed with every remark he made, stopping him dead. Nor were Mrs. Coates or the unknown man—presumably husband to the unknown woman— much help in the middle of that side. Mr. Harriman, between Mrs. Coates and Mrs. Cushing, did laugh at Mrs. Cushing's sallies and Mr. Avery's anecdotes, but contributed almost nothing himself.

In short, the party was a failure. Hilda shifted from one foot to the other and wished everyone would go home.

Perhaps Mrs. George felt the same way. At any rate, she was not long in giving the signal to the ladies to retire to the drawing room. That meant that Hilda, too, could withdraw, though it provided her no respite. She still had to help serve coffee and sweets, and the drawing room, up one flight on the main floor, was much hotter than the semi-basement dining room, even with all the windows open to their fullest extent. The ladies brought their fans out of their décolletages and plied them listlessly.

"Surely the weather will break soon," said Mrs. Cushing, accepting a bonbon from Hilda and declining a cup of coffee from Norah. "It's been a terrible summer for the farmers."

"The weather has been good for Mr. Warren," commented Mrs. Warren timidly. "He's been able to keep his men working on the new city hall with almost no interruptions."

"I'm sure that must be a great satisfaction to you," said Mrs. Avery in a high, affected tone, waving both Hilda and Norah away. "Especially as he works right along with them. Such dedication! Now, Mr. Avery is always very careful to keep out of the hot sun, himself. He finds it enervating. He would much rather buy land for others to build on than do the work himself."

After a nasty second of silence, three women started to talk at once—but not to Mrs. Avery. Women, Hilda had noticed at other parties, didn't much enjoy talking with Mrs. Avery, though they were ready enough to listen to some new piece of gossip. She excelled at gossip, especially the ill-natured variety. Norah caught Hilda's eye and mouthed a silent "meow." Hilda stifled a giggle.

The men didn't linger long downstairs, perhaps because no port or brandy was served in that teetotal household, and even a cigar loses its savor when one knows that an impatient woman is waiting. Or perhaps it was simply that their conversation was no more interesting after dinner than it had been earlier. At any rate, Hilda had only a few more minutes to stand on her sore feet before the husbands came up the grand staircase in little groups of two and three, nobody saying much.

They continued to say little over coffee, and at last, at last, men began to nod to their wives and make the little gestures that meant they were ready to leave. Hilda and Norah, more than ready themselves for the evening to end, were released. Norah went down to the kitchen to help with the cleanup, while Hilda hurried upstairs to fetch the light scarves and shawls that the women had worn, not because they were needed, but because one did not go out on the street without a wrap of some sort over one's evening clothes.

Mr. Williams was ready with the men's top hats. As the couples paired off, gave their flowery thanks to their host and hostess, and prepared to take themselves out the door, Hilda saw Mr. Avery and Mr. Warren pass near each other, getting their hats.

"Well, Warren, are you ready to sell me that piece of land yet? It's doing you no good, you know."

"I've told you before, I don't want to sell that land."

"Oh, but Herbert!" It was Mrs. Avery, suddenly at her husband's side with a pretty pout on her face. "You promised me a country house out there!"

"You see, Warren? When the ladies take a fancy to something, what's to be done? Oh, well, you'll change your mind sooner or later. Just think about it, that's all I ask. Extra money is very useful, you know. Just think how your lovely wife would look in a new gown. And diamonds, perhaps?"

He had turned to smile brilliantly at Mrs. Warren, who smiled back and then recoiled at the black look on her husband's face.

"Leave my wife out of this, Avery!" Mr. Warren turned his back on Mr. Avery so rapidly that he nearly stepped on the other man's narrow, well-shod feet. He grasped his wife's elbow without a word and steered her, or pushed her, toward the door.

Hilda watched it all, secure in the knowledge that as a servant she was invisible. She watched the Averys leave, he proud and solicitous of his beautiful wife, she simpering. Mr. Avery was, Hilda thought, the sort of man who would always be charming to women, even unremarkable ones like Mrs. Warren. She watched the Harrimans, little Mr. Harriman following in his wife's wake like a tugboat trailing after an ocean liner.

Mr. and Mrs. Coates left in the silence they had maintained all night, enveloped in a shell of self-satisfaction. The Slicks hurried off as soon as courtesy permitted, as did the couple

Hilda didn't know, both with the air of a duty now fortunately over and done with. The Singlers lingered, hearty and agreeable, lacking the sense to take themselves off until Mr. Williams pointedly handed Mr. Singler his hat and said, "Your carriage is waiting, sir."

The Cushings stayed for a few minutes to exchange a last word or two with the Studebakers, a chuckle or wry grimace at the way the evening had gone, but at last they, too, stepped out the door, which Mr. Williams would not close and lock until all the guests were out of sight. Nor would he breathe a sigh of relief. Mr. Williams was very well trained.

Outside in the drive, the last bored coachmen waited to bring carriages up under the porte cochere. They and the horses were ready for home, too.

2

Dastardly Act . . .
—South Bend *Tribune*, September 6, 1901

APART from the dinner party, August was a very dull month at Tippecanoe Place. The owners of the house, Mr. and Mrs. Clement Studebaker, had been in Europe since May, traveling in leisurely fashion, in search of better health for Mr. Clem. Their son and daughter-in-law entertained far less than the elder Studebakers, so Hilda's work proceeded according to routine. So routine, in fact, that she was growing bored when the telegram came near the end of the month, and life picked up again.

"They are returning home!" Mr. Williams announced at breakfast. "They will leave next week, and expect to be home in time for their wedding anniversary on the thirteenth."

The servants knew what that meant. By the end of the following week, Hilda was longing for her former boredom.

"The cushion is not clean, Hilda! Just look at that spot." The butler pointed an accusing finger.

"I have just cleaned it, Mr. Williams. The spot is in the pattern," she replied tartly. "Mrs. George made a mistake when she worked the tapestry. I heard her say—"

"That will do, Hilda. It is not for you to correct me, nor to criticize your employer's handiwork. Take it away, and make sure it is thoroughly dry before you replace it on the love seat. The weather has been most sultry; we cannot risk mildew. And tell Anton to bring me the silver dish covers, one at a time or he might scratch them, and he is not to forget his gloves."

Gritting her teeth, Hilda turned to leave the butler's pantry.

"Hilda!"

She turned back.

"Answer me when I give you an order!"

"Yes, Mr. Williams. Will that be all, Mr. Williams?"

He glared at her, suspecting insolence under her controlled tone, but her face was ironed smooth. He snorted. "Oh, be off with you, and don't dillydally!"

This time she escaped. Muttering highly improper Swedish under her breath, she crossed the hall to the kitchen and poked her head in the door.

"Mrs. Sullivan, where is Anton?"

The cook's head and shoulders were in one of the ovens. She continued to scrub, her voice muffled and irritable. "And how would I know that? Off somewheres loafin' when he ought to be tendin' to his job, likely as not. He's not here where he could be some use, I know that."

Hilda went upstairs to the main floor and deposited the cushion carefully on the love seat in the family sitting room. "Be sure that you do not touch that cushion when you come down, Maria," she said sternly, looking up at an under housemaid who was standing on a ladder in the middle of the room polishing the gas chandelier. "It is clean, and I do not want soot on it from your fingers. Have you seen Anton?"

"I think he's upstairs, miss. There was trouble with the taps in one of the bathrooms."

Hilda ascended the grand staircase, taking care to step lightly. The stair carpet had been taken up and was even now being beaten soundly in the backyard by another of the dailies, and the bared oak stair treads must not be scarred.

Eventually she found the footman, not in one of the second-floor bathrooms, but on the third floor, lubricating the latch on a guest-room door.

"He wants you," she said briefly. "You are to take to him the silver dish covers. One at a time, he said, and wear your gloves.

And you must wash your hands first," she added, looking at his blackened fingers with disapproval.

Anton, the footman, was at sixteen the youngest daily servant regularly employed at the great house. Accustomed to being ordered around, he resignedly abandoned one job to look after another. Hilda took a moment to stop in her bedroom near the back stairs and wash her face, hoping to cool off a little.

She dropped down on the edge of her bed with a sigh. She hadn't needed Mr. Williams to tell her that the weather was sultry. August's heat had continued unabated. She felt she was being broiled alive in her long black uniform, and her feet in their tightly buttoned boots felt like frizzling sausages, just ready to pop. She longed to take the boots off and wiggle her toes, but she knew she'd never get them on again, and she didn't even care to consider what Mr. Williams would say if she went about her work in stockinged feet.

Anyone might have thought the place had been allowed to stand empty and neglected, thought Hilda resentfully. Mr. Williams, who was inclined to lose his head in a crisis, was issuing orders with the rapid fire of a telegraph machine, and everything that could be cleaned or polished was being cleaned or polished within an inch of its life. The ship carrying the master and mistress was due in New York on Sunday, but no one was quite sure when they would arrive in South Bend, so preparations were reaching the point of frenzy.

The one bright spot in the whole situation was that Colonel and Mrs. George had taken their young son, George Jr., back to school, and had then spent a few days visiting friends on the way home. Their absence meant that the servants could work uninterrupted for a change, not having to bother with proper meals or worry about making noise and mess where it might discommode the family.

The blessing, thought Hilda sourly as she got to her feet, was mixed. As head housemaid she was run ragged, but at least she had plenty of assistance. Because of the need for haste, every daily ever employed at Tippecanoe Place, and a few new ones, had been called in to help. Colonel and Mrs. George were expected back tomorrow evening, Saturday, on the 8:37 train, and all the big jobs had to be done by then.

"Excuse me, miss." A scared little Irish scullery maid of thirteen or so, brought in to help clean the kitchen, stood in the doorway, her hands pleating her apron. "I wouldn't've bothered you, but Mr. Williams, he said as he wanted you downstairs."

"It is not your fault," said Hilda, summoning up a gracious smile. After all, given the complexity of Irish families, the child might very well be one of Norah's relatives, or Mrs. Sullivan's, or even Patrick Cavanaugh's. Patrick was the handsome fireman who was not—quite definitely not—Hilda's gentleman friend, only a friend, and she had never met his family. At any rate, there was no reason to be cross with—Eileen, was it? Hilda rather enjoyed condescending to her underlings on the rare occasions when she got the chance.

Besides, if Hilda was pleasant, little Eileen probably wouldn't tell Mr. Williams she had found Hilda resting in her room. She restrained herself from patting the girl on the head as she followed her down the service stairs to see what Mr. Williams wanted now.

On an ordinary day, Hilda, who rose at five-thirty and was expected to have a good many chores completed before breakfast an hour later, was allowed a rest of an hour or so after lunch. Not today. Lunch was a cold, hurried meal, snatched when opportunity afforded. Hilda ate some ham and a couple of cold potatoes washed down with water, and went on to her next job, the painstaking cleaning of the tall cupboards in the butler's pantry. Mr. Williams dealt personally with the silver, of course, but all the precious china and crystal had to be removed and carefully washed in the pantry sink, and then the shelves themselves must be relined with fresh paper and the glass doors washed before the fragile treasures were replaced. The task was always Hilda's responsibility, but it was usually done a shelf or two at a time over a period of several days. This time Hilda had persuaded Mr. Williams to let Norah help her.

"For it is not a thing I can hurry," she had explained. "I might drop a plate and break it. And it is quicker and easier with two, when one can climb the ladder and take things out to give to the other."

Permission had been grudging, but now Norah and Hilda were working together for the first time all day.

"How're you holdin' up, girl?" Norah asked, sticking out her lower lip and blowing a stream of air upward to try to dislodge the damp hair that was straggling over her brow. Both her hands were occupied with a heavy Spode platter.

Hilda, up on the ladder putting away the contents of the top shelf, sighed gustily. "I am very tired. And I am very hot. Never, never when I come to this country do I imagine it will be so hot. At night when I cannot sleep for the heat I dream of Björka, of the winter nights with the snow, and the clear, cold air . . . and the stars, Norah, the stars so near you can touch them, almost, and so bright. . . ." She sighed again.

Norah snorted. "Huh! And you catchin' your death in that drafty little house of yours. I'll take the heat, thank you. We may get worked to death here in America, but you and me, we'll never freeze to death. Here, be careful with this. It weighs a ton."

With infinite care Hilda took the ornately decorated platter in her gloved hands and set it upright at the back of the shelf. "Those bowls now. No, do not stack them like that! Napkins must go between so they will not scratch or chip. The ones from the top drawer, there."

They worked their way steadily through one section of cupboard shelves, but Norah rebelled when they were ready to start on the second.

"I'm gettin' meself out of this uniform and into me coolest skirt and waist, and I don't care what His Almightiness says! I'm drippin' wet, and I'm goin' to wash and get cool. There's no one here to care what I wear, anyhow."

Privately, Hilda agreed with her, but she was so hot she felt it unlikely a mere change of clothes would help. Surely, though, Mr. Williams wouldn't grudge her a few minutes outside where there might be a stray breeze.

There was in fact almost no breeze at all. She found a shady bench at the back of the property and sat, fanning herself with her apron. It was *hot*. It had been hot and dry nearly all summer. The Studebaker lawns looked green and cool, true, but only because of Frank Czeszewski's unremitting toil. Czeszewski was the head gardener, a surly fellow whom Hilda disliked, but even she had to admit he worked hard. She could see him now, moving a sprinkler down by the far corner of the front lawn and getting wet in the spray. Hilda envied him.

She stopped moving her apron. The gusts of hot air she was creating weren't worth the effort. She felt as wilted as the flags that hung limply here and there from front-porch roofs, flags that had been hung out for Labor Day on Monday and hadn't been taken down. Hilda rubbed her temples. Much more of this heat wave and she was going to start having her headaches again.

Even the sounds of a busy Friday afternoon in the city—horses' hooves and iron wheels on the brick and cedar-block pavements, voices raised in greeting or argument, the happy squeals of children, the barking of dogs—seemed muted today. Autumn might be nearly upon them, but the feel of the day was that of lazy, languid summer.

Then Hilda heard a high, strident cry, a harsh sound of alarm, a frightened, confused tumult drawing ever nearer. Curious, she stood and moved to where she could see the street.

People were running and shouting. Was it a fire? She saw no smoke, heard no clang of bells from fire trucks. The running seemed to be directionless. Except—yes, leading the spread of agitation were two newsboys from the *Times,* coming down the street at a dead run and shouting the news as they came.

"Assassination! President shot! Assassination! President is dying! Assassination! Assassination!"

Hilda ran to the street corner, seized a paper from the panting boy, and ran back to the house, sobbing as she went.

"Mr. Williams! Mr. Williams! Look, look, a terrible t'ing—"

"HILDA JOHANSSON! Control yourself!" roared Mr. Williams as he reached for the paper. "Nothing can be so—great God in heaven!"

✦

As the shock wave spread through the four stories of the great house, normal life was suspended. The dailies were sent home to deal with their distress in the bosom of their families, while the live-in staff sat in the servants' room weeping and speculating endlessly. Even Mr. Williams's bulldog, Rex, seemed to mourn, lying listlessly near his master's chair, chin on his front paws.

The information in the extra edition, a stop-press block on the front page, was meager in the extreme. Even in the regular evening editions of both papers, the *Times* and the *Tribune,* there was little more real news. President McKinley had been shot twice in the stomach that afternoon while attending the Pan-American Exposition in Buffalo, New York. He was alive, but in grave condition in a hospital. "HIS WOUNDS ARE FATAL," screamed the second headline in the *Tribune,* but there were no details. Nothing was known about his attacker.

"It'll be them strikers in Pittsburgh," said Mrs. Sullivan darkly. "Antichrists, the lot of them!"

"And what," asked John Bolton, the coachman, "would strikers from Pittsburgh be doing in Buffalo? They've the price of a fare, have they? And if it's 'anarchists' you mean, why wouldn't they be? What's the government ever done for them but put them down and take the bread out of their children's mouths?"

Norah nodded in half approval, but Mr. Williams was wroth.

"You ought to be ashamed of yourself, John Bolton! Here's our president, a noble man, beloved by all, dying from an assassin's bullet and you sit there praising the anarchists! You should be put in jail yourself!"

"I didn't praise them!" John retorted. "I don't go so far as to say the government ought to be done away with, and I'm as sorry as any of you about the president. But I do say the government does nothing for the workingman, and needs to be changed. If the Democrats were in—"

He was interrupted by a loud knock on the back door. Rex lifted his head and uttered a low growl. Looking both alarmed and annoyed, Mr. Williams went to the door at the bottom of the set of outside steps leading up from the semi-basement. "Who is it?"

"It is Anton, sir. There is news. I thought you would want to know."

The footman was hurried into the servants' room with scant ceremony. "Well, boy?" demanded Mr. Williams.

"I have been waiting at the telegraph office, sir, for any news. Some of it is good. President McKinley is resting well, and the doctors think now that he will live through the night, at least." There were murmurs of relief, and Anton's pale cheeks took on a little color. It was seldom that he occupied center stage. "But there is more exciting news than that. The assassin was captured by the crowd and is now in the hands of the police. He said at first his name was Fred Nieman—that means 'no man' in German—but that is not his real name, and he is not a German. He is a Pole, a man named Leon Czolgosz."

Anton, who was from Prussia, stumbled over the difficult name. He tried to appear shocked, but he was obviously relieved that it was a Pole rather than a German who had been arrested for the heinous crime. In the hubbub over the news, Hilda was the only one to notice the extremely startled look that passed across the face of John Bolton.

3

Cleveland
... perhaps the plot to kill the president was hatched in
this city.

—South Bend *Tribune,* September 7, 1901

No one in the Studebaker mansion slept much that night. For that matter, sleep was lost all over the city, all over the nation. In Buffalo, anxious doctors kept vigil at the bedside of the most important man in the country. In Washington, shocked legislators and government officials tried to make plans. On a farm near Cleveland, a grindingly poor Polish man and his wife offered despairing prayers for the president and for their son, now in the hands of the police. Everywhere the pious prayed and the unbelieving worried. In a few carefully hidden rooms, widely scattered across the country, men gathered in bitter rejoicing.

In several houses in South Bend, men sweated with fear, and in at least one, a man lay awake and worried.

John Bolton lay sleepless in his carriage-house bedroom for a long time. Adept at sliding out from under hard work, he wasn't particularly tired, and it was necessary that he think things out carefully.

The small room was hot and smelled of the stables below, but it was neither the heat nor the odor that disturbed him. He was in trouble.

Not, he thought, such deep trouble that he couldn't wiggle out, if he were shrewd and cautious. Cautious! The very idea was inimical to his nature. If only he could go away for a few weeks . . . but that was impossible unless he gave up his job entirely.

He swore softly in the night and one of the horses in the stalls below whinnied uneasily.

Hilda slept fitfully. She was young and strong, and very tired from hard work and the draining effect of shock and grief. Sleep was not to be denied. But the stifling heat at the top of the house made her restless, and her dreams were full of vague terrors.

When her alarm clock rang at five-thirty, she put her pillow over her head and let the shrill clamor ring itself out. She felt as though she'd had no sleep at all, and she would have liked to turn over and bury herself in the bedclothes.

But Norah, awake next door, banged on the wall. "Out o' bed, then, me girl. The family's comin' home today, and it's double work for us all!"

There was no help for it. Hilda muttered something in Swedish and dragged herself out of her damp and rumpled bed.

The talk at the breakfast table, when she got there after a furious hour of dusting and brushing and scrubbing, was of one subject only. South Bend was now without a morning paper, the *Times* having decided to publish in the afternoon, but Anton had stopped by the telegraph office on his way to Tippecanoe Place and was able to pass along some news. It was guardedly reassuring, at least as to the president's condition. He'd passed a reasonably comfortable night, but his temperature was 102 and his pulse and respiration were rapid.

"At least he's still alive," said Norah in a mournful voice. That seemed to sum it up. Mrs. Sullivan sniffled and Mr. Williams blew his nose, trumpeting into a large white handkerchief. Its sole use under normal circumstances was to adorn his breast pocket, and it was a measure of his distress that he used it at all. He looked confused to find it in his hand, shook his head, and stuffed it into a trousers pocket.

"Where there's life, there's hope," said John Bolton. His voice was free of any hint of sarcasm, and Mr. Williams nodded at him approvingly.

"That's a much more proper attitude, lad."

John scowled like a small boy being complimented by a maiden aunt. "Was there any news about the Polish man?" he asked Anton.

"Not that I heard. The police have him in the sweatbox, someone said. I could go and find out." He looked eagerly at the butler, who frowned and shook his head.

"We are all anxious for news, but the work of the household cannot be neglected. There is no time to waste." Then, perhaps in sympathy with the doleful faces around the table, he cleared his throat. "When the grocer's boy comes, and the butcher's, I will pass along what news they bring. Now we must all see to our jobs."

No one was in the mood to work, but servants are not expected to surrender to their moods. There were yesterday afternoon's tasks to be done, as well as today's, before the arrival of Colonel and Mrs. George. As soon as Hilda and Norah had flown through their regular morning chores, entrusting as much of the work as possible to the dailies, they picked up their pantry cleaning where they had left off after yesterday's terrible news. Norah, who liked to chatter when they worked together, was unusually silent, speaking only when Hilda asked her a question, and not always then.

At first Hilda enjoyed the quiet. They seemed to get through more work when they didn't talk, for one thing, and besides, there were things Hilda wanted to think about. But as noon approached, and the day's heat became more and more oppressive even here in the semi-basement, Hilda's nerves began to wear thin.

"Norah," she said sharply.

Norah said nothing, but turned a set face to Hilda.

"We will stop work now, and finish after lunch."

That did bring a startled response. "But we've nearly finished! There's only the one shelf, and it with just the two punch bowls."

"We will stop *now*." Hilda was not in any sense Norah's boss, but something in her voice kept Norah from making that point. She eyed Hilda warily.

"We will go outside, and we will hang up the wet dish towels, and we will talk."

"You can hang up the towels, if it's a break you want. I'll finish here by meself."

"No," said Hilda, and there was steel in her voice. "You will come with me."

Rebellion flared in Norah's black eyes, but she picked up a pile of damp towels and marched out the back door.

"Now," said Hilda with determination when the two had reached the clothesline. "You will tell me what it is that worries you. You can talk here and no one will hear you."

Norah muttered something and began to pin towels to the line.

"Norah Murphy, talk to me! When I am in a temper, when I am afraid or upset, always, always you make me talk to you, if I want to talk or if I do not. And always I feel better when I talk to you, because you are my friend. Now you are upset and you will talk to me, if you want to or not. You *will!*" Hilda stamped her foot and then cried out. Her boots really were too tight for hot weather. "Now see what you have done! I hurt my foot, and all because you have become a—a crab!"

Norah snorted. "A clam, you'll maybe be meanin'? An' is it my fault if you lose that Swedish temper?"

"Yes, thank you, a clam, that is what shuts tight and does not open up, *ja?* And yes, it is your fault because you make me worry, but now you will tell me and it will be all right. Here, sit on the bench. There is some shade, and Mr. Williams cannot see us here."

Norah sighed and sat, most of the fight gone out of her. Her face was grim as she looked at Hilda.

"I'd think you'd know about not wantin' to talk. Once I had to near thrash you before you'd talk, because you were afraid. And oh, Hilda, it's afraid I am now!" Her control broke. Tears started in her eyes; she let them flow unchecked.

"It is because of this terrible thing, *ja*? This shooting of the president?"

Norah nodded dumbly.

"But Norah—what is it to do with you? We are all sad, but . . ."

Norah sniffed and wiped her eyes. "Maybe it's nothing to do with me, at all. And maybe it is, and that's what's got me so scairt." She sniffed again. "It's me brother Flynn, you see. He's the oldest, you know, and always the wildest. And he's got in with a bunch o' men at the mills that're talkin' strikes an' that."

"What mills? I thought he worked at the Oliver factory."

"He left there and went to the woolen mills, oh, months ago. He said the pay was better, but I think he just wanted a change. He's always gettin' bored and changin' jobs."

"That is not good," said Hilda, her stern Lutheran creed coming to the fore. "It is better to be steady."

"I know." Norah sighed. "I've told him, and Mother's told him, but nobody can tell Flynn anything. He's not bad, you know, just headstrong. He has these men to the house sometimes, and I've heard 'em talkin'." Her eyes brimmed over again. "Hilda, they're sayin' wild things! The one that talks the most, the ringleader—his name is Kapinski, Joseph Kapinski—he says the labor unions in town don't do enough for the workin' man, 'specially the immigrants, and they've got to take things in their own hands."

"A strike?"

"And not just a strike! Hilda, I've heard 'em say things about burnin' the mills if they don't get what they want! When they get to drinkin' . . ." She broke down in sobs, and Hilda took her hand.

"You are afraid they will talk anarchy, *ja*?"

"I'm afraid maybe they already have, when I didn't hear! And, Hilda, it's true the police don't like us Irish, anyway, nor the Poles, neither. You know it's true. If they get wind of what's in the air now, now when they are looking for someone to blame, anyone . . ." She buried her face in her hands.

Hilda had no comfort to offer. It was all too likely that the authorities would have small tolerance for anyone even remotely connected with anarchical sentiment just now.

"I will finish in the pantry myself, Norah," she offered. "If you want to leave for a little while, to see your family, I will make up a lie to tell Mr. Williams."

"No, it's all right." Norah gulped, blew her nose, and stood up shakily. "I'll just wash me face and have a lie down instead o' lunch. I'll be fine. You were right, Hilda. I feel better for talkin' about it."

Hilda wasn't sure *she* felt better for hearing it.

The day dragged on. Hilda finished in the pantry alone after all. Mr. Williams had set Norah to work in the dining room, polishing the thousands of brass nails that held the Moroccan leather wall hangings in place. It was a job Norah hated, and one that had to be done frequently, since only a soft cloth and elbow grease could be used. The usual brass cleaning methods, involving sweet oil and finely powdered rottenstone, would have ruined the leather. She had plenty of help from the dailies, but the job still took the rest of the afternoon.

By six o'clock everything was done and everyone was exhausted. The casual dailies were paid and dismissed, while Anton and Elsie and the live-in servants gathered in a weary, dispirited group around their supper table, too tired and hot to do more than pick at their food. John Bolton slid in, late as usual, and he brought the evening papers with him.

"News!" he said, holding them aloft.

It seemed to Hilda that the room itself held its breath for a moment. Mrs. Sullivan, white faced, finally spoke the question aloud.

"Good news, or bad?"

"Not bad. He's holdin' his own, they say."

Eager hands reached for the papers, but Mr. Williams cleared his throat.

"The papers must be kept fresh for Colonel George," he said pompously. "Remember that he will be home in a few hours, and will wish to read them. Give them to me, John, and I will read the important parts aloud before I iron the papers."

He was maddeningly slow about it, scanning the front page

silently for several minutes, but at last he cleared his throat and began to dole out tidbits. The president's condition was no worse. Mrs. McKinley had been allowed to see him. The assassin, Czolgosz, was quoted as saying, "I shot him for an example, and I hope he dies."

The servants murmured angrily.

"Let me see if there is any more about him, the villain." The butler rustled the pages of the *Tribune*, radiating magisterial importance. "Ah, yes, this is of interest. He is from Cleveland, apparently, this Czolgosz, or however you say the dastard's name. Hmm . . .'letter of recommendation signed by a Cleveland man,' it says they found on his person . . . ah! Listen to this! 'On Czolgosz were also found several names and addresses of Cleveland parties. One was number 170 Superior Street. This number has been the meeting place of anarchistic societies.' Anarchists! Think of it!"

"I knew it!" said Mrs. Sullivan with a snort. "All them strikers in Chicago, and on the railroads, too—no good will come of it, you mark my words."

"Evil has already come of it," said Mr. Williams portentously, and at that John Bolton exploded.

" 'Ow many times do I 'ave to tell you?" he shouted, reverting in his agitation to the accent he was born with. "The strikers are NOT anarchists, only decent workin' men tryin' to get the money they break their backs for! And if it weren't for the strike-breakin' scum 'ired by the bosses, takin' their jobs away and leavin' them to starve—"

"ENOUGH!" Mr. Williams slammed his fist on the table. A cup skittered to the floor with a crash. Rex woke up and whined, the kitchen cat prudently took itself elsewhere, and Elsie, the scullery maid, uttered a little shriek. "I will not have such radical talk in this house. Men who work hard have no need to complain; those who would rather laze away their days and whine have no place in a civilized society. If you wish to sympathize with strikers, John Bolton, you may find yourself another position. And how, may I ask, do you come to know so much about it, you who know very little about hard work?"

"You're not the only one in this household who reads the newspaper, you know." John's face was sullen and defiant, but he had his *h*'s back under control. "And how many stables have you ever mucked out, to lecture me about hard, dirty work?" The last comment was made under his breath as he stomped out the door, but Hilda heard it.

Mrs. Sullivan, who was used to the butler's temper tantrums and thought them insignificant compared with the ones she herself could throw now and again, reached for the newspaper Mr. Williams had thrown down in his fury. She wasn't a great reader, but this was exciting stuff; she didn't intend to wait to be handed bits of information. Breathing heavily, she ran her finger along the lines of type and mouthed words as she labored over the text.

"Saints preserve us!"

"What is it, Mrs. Sullivan? I'd thank you to give the paper back to me, *if* you please."

"You wasn't readin' it, was you, then? But how you come to miss this, I'll never know."

She handed it over, pointing.

It was at the end of the story about Czolgosz, relating an interview with his stepmother (through an interpreter, since the woman did not speak English).

" 'Leon left home about sixty days ago,' " Mr. Williams read aloud. " 'We heard from him a few weeks ago. He was then in Indiana. He wrote as he was going away, stating in all probability we would not see him again.' The woman failed to recollect the name of the Indiana city."

Norah turned white; Hilda thought her friend was going to faint, but nothing could be said in front of everyone else. Elsie, the somewhat slow scullery maid, looked puzzled.

"Who's Leon?" she asked. "And why do you care if he was in Indiana weeks ago?"

Mrs. Sullivan's laugh was a trifle shrill. "Fool of a girl! Leon's the assassin! I can't say his last name right, but that's his Christian name, if you can call someone like that a Christian. And he's Polish. Does that mean nothin' to you, girl?"

"No," said Elsie simply.

Hilda wished for Norah's sake that they would leave it at that, but Mr. Williams tut-tutted over Elsie's stupidity. "There are a great many Poles in South Bend, Elsie," he explained with an elaborate display of patience. "Perhaps more than in any other Indiana city. It is unfortunately somewhat likely that it was here the assassin was visiting."

Elsie got it at last. "Oh, but that woulda been terrible! We'd of woke up one morning, mebbe, and found all our throats cut!"

The others laughed, but Hilda was unable even to smile.

When they had given up all pretense of eating and Mr. Williams had sent them to their rooms to clean up before the family arrived home, Hilda and Norah were able to talk.

"Try not to worry so much, Norah! We do not *know* that he was here."

"But if he was? And if our Flynn met him?"

"Would he tell you, if you ask?"

"No. He won't talk to me, not since I gave him the rough side of me tongue about it all. Oh, Hilda, I have to know! I have to know what may be comin'!"

"Then," said Hilda with sudden resolve, "I will find out for you. I am good with questions, to make people tell me things. And I know where I will begin."

"You'll be careful, Hilda, now! There's danger—"

"There is danger, yes, but for me it is the danger of the roving hands and the glad eye."

Norah frowned. "What're you talkin' about, then?"

"I talk about John Bolton, and soon, I will talk to him. I do not gamble, Norah, but if I did I would make a large bet that he knows much more about that terrible assassin than he should."

4

Mexican Headache Cure
A splitting headache cured immediately. . . . It is perfectly
harmless, no bad results follow its use . . .
—Sears, Roebuck & Co. catalogue, 1900

A s she washed and changed into a fresh uniform (wishing
rebelliously that she needn't put on anything more
constricting than a nightdress, so hot and sticky was the
evening), Hilda tried to think of a way to approach John. She
had joked about roving hands to Norah, but truly the problem
was a serious one that had to be handled carefully, despite the
urgency of her need to talk to him. Anything resembling a
rendezvous must be avoided, because she was certain that John
would misinterpret her intentions and take advantage of the
situation.

That must not happen, and not simply because Hilda would
be irritated and embarrassed. She was fully aware that she
would be blamed if things got out of hand. Unfair as it was, a
woman who lost her reputation always bore the brunt of the
punishment, even if she had been forcibly seduced. In Hilda's
case, it would mean losing her job, with scant possibility of
finding another in any but the most menial drudgery—or worse.

She thought it wouldn't come to that. She thought she
could deal with John. But she couldn't take the risk. No,
somehow she must find a way to speak to him privately without
seeming to invite flirtation.

She still hadn't solved her problem when it was solved for

her, and true to her contrary nature, she wasn't particularly grateful.

She was just slipping into her long black skirt when Mr. Williams knocked at her door, fussy and impatient.

"Are you not dressed yet, Hilda? You must hurry; we will leave in a few minutes."

"Leave?" said Hilda blankly.

"For the station. You will come with us, of course. Mrs. George will be tired from her travels and in need of assistance, and you know that there is no ladies' maid available, as Michelle is accompanying Mrs. Clem. You will have to come, so tidy yourself and be quick about it!"

Just for a moment Hilda saw red. Mrs. George would be tired, would she? Had *she* risen before dawn and worked all day in blistering heat? Had *she* scrubbed and polished and climbed up and down ladders at the bidding of a carping butler? Was *her* head beginning to feel as if someone were inside pounding hammers against the brain?

But there was nothing to be gained by losing her temper. Mrs. George was a lady and Hilda was a servant, and all the rage she could muster wouldn't change the hierarchy of the world. It was, perhaps, just as well Mr. Williams couldn't see the flash in her blue eyes. In that brief moment, Hilda had had a glimpse of sympathetic understanding for the strikers and the anarchists.

Then she shrugged. At least she would get a ride in one of the fine carriages. Mr. Clem, president of Studebaker Brothers, used only the best of his products for himself and his family.

It was only when she found herself on the high seat of the elegant open landau next to the splendidly arrayed coachman that she began to appreciate her luck.

"You're a lucky girl and no mistake," John said as they trotted off to the Chicago and Southern station. "Privileged to ride up here next to the handsomest man in South Bend!"

"That will be enough of that talk, John Bolton," said Hilda severely. "I did not choose to sit here. And I wish to talk to you seriously, so be quiet and let me speak."

Her voice was tense and very low. Mr. Williams, sitting on

the backseat, would be able to hear normal speech. John looked at her with a frown.

"And what do you think is so important that you have to whisper to me?" His voice held arrogance, and something else. Anger? Apprehension?

"I wish to know what you know about the assassin's visit to South Bend."

The reins jerked in John's hands. The horses shied; the carriage swayed. From behind them came the butler's angry voice: "Mind what you're about, John Bolton!"

"And just what makes you think I know anything about that?" John's voice was low and angry.

"You do not say it did not happen," Hilda whispered, with some satisfaction.

"And I don't say it did, either!"

"But you know it did. You were there."

This time John had himself under control. His hands tightened on the reins; that was all.

"If you know so much about it, you tell me what happened."

"I do not know. But you do. John, you show the truth to anyone who watches you. No one, I think, no one but me, has yet noticed. But you do not have the good face to hide your thoughts. You must tell me, and we must think what to do."

"Giving me orders now, are you, Miss Prim?"

Hilda tossed her head. A few wisps of golden hair escaped her coronet braids; she wore only her cap, not a proper hat. "You will, I think, get into trouble without some help. And not only you. There are others—Norah's brother, perhaps."

"Oh, yes?" This time there was a hint of menace behind the words. "And maybe a few more of the Irish, as well. Maybe someone you know, named Patrick?"

"No!" The word rang out. Mr. Williams glared at Hilda's back and a man in the street looked up at her, astonishment and concern on his face.

"Are you all right, miss?" he called out, but the carriage had already passed by and turned the corner.

"So that surprises you, does it?" said John. "You'd best keep quiet about it, don't you think?"

"I do not believe it," said Hilda flatly. "Patrick is sensible. He would not involve himself in what is against the law. You say this to make me angry."

John, ignoring the horses for a moment, looked at her with dark intensity. "What I say, my dear, is that you'd best tend to your dusting and not go meddling in what you don't understand. I know what I'm doing, and I don't intend to get into trouble. I don't need your help, or anybody else's. This is men's business, and don't you forget it or you'll be sorry!"

He slapped the reins against the horses' flanks. The carriage jerked, and Hilda had to hold tight to keep her seat.

All the rest of the way to the station, and all the way home, riding next to Mrs. George to tend to her needs, Hilda seethed. She had been trying to help, to learn what she could and also to save John from his own indiscretion. She had not believed it was anything worse than that. Now she was uncertain. Was he acting mysterious simply because she was a woman, and therefore unfit, in his eyes, to know about serious matters? Or was there something more, something worse?

And was there, oh, Herre Gud, was there any chance that Patrick really was involved?

Mrs. Sullivan had prepared an elaborate late supper in honor of the family's return. She took grave offense when nobody ate much. "Williams," Mrs. George had said, "please tell Mrs. Sullivan everything was delicious, but no one has any appetite in this heat. Tell her I'd be grateful if she'd put the chicken in the icebox; perhaps we can have a salad for lunch tomorrow."

Mrs. Sullivan was not appeased. "Hmph! Askin' *me* to serve leftovers! Me that's cooked for the best families in Boston! Next they'll be tellin' me to order in the meals from the Oliver Hotel. Don't know why they bother havin' a cook at all. *She* fancies herself a cook, all that chafin' dish muck she messes about with, let *her* do the cookin' for others to pick at!" And more of the same, insulting Mrs. George's culinary abilities and pointing out her own unappreciated excellence until Hilda, who was exhausted and whose head was hurting more and more, was ready to scream.

At last the scorned meal was tidied away, the last dish washed and put away, the kitchen floor scrubbed (that fell to poor Elsie's lot), the stove damped down for the night. The doors were all locked, the household ready for their well-earned rest. Now that she could fall into bed, however, Hilda knew that she would not sleep. "Mr. Williams," she said, "my head will split in two unless I get some fresh air. I must sit outside for a little. I will lock the back door."

The butler's procedure for locking up was sacred and inviolable. Hilda had never before dared such a request; now she phrased it as a demand. The butler opened his mouth for a severe scolding, but Hilda's eyes were closed. Her face was white and damp with sweat, her breathing shallow. Plainly, she was really ill.

"I should think you'd do better in bed," he said, frowning. "Or perhaps Mrs. Sullivan has a powder you could take."

"The powders do no good, and it is so hot upstairs I could not sleep. Please, if I can just sit where it is dark and cooler, just for a few minutes, I can sleep then, I t'ink." She swayed, and Norah put out a concerned hand.

"I'll sit with 'er, Mr. Williams. Only for a while, to cool off, and then we'll both come in."

Mr. Williams was tired, too. Thoughts about what could happen with those two out together at night passed through his mind, but it was only the backyard, after all, and even he could see that Hilda was in no condition for mischief tonight.

"Very well," he said stiffly. "For fifteen minutes, no more. And mind you put the chain on the door; I don't trust that new Yale lock. I hope you feel better, Hilda," he added grudgingly.

Though the air outside still clung to the face like wet flannel, a hot, fitful breeze had sprung up, bringing with it the faint scent of rain. Dark, irregular shadows skidded across the moon, and now and then the whole sky brightened briefly with heat lightning. The crickets chirped their rapid-fire temperature report, and the cicadas buzzed as loudly as in mid-August, but the weather was changing. Hilda was glad of it; the farmers needed rain badly after the long drought, and she herself panted for relief from the heat.

Norah led Hilda to the stone bench just off the back drive that was their favorite resting place. It was lit only dimly by the distant electric streetlight down on the corner of the large property. "That'll be cool to sit on, anyhow. And I brought a wet rag for your head. Now let me take off them boots—no, don't try to do it yourself. Bendin' over'll make your head throb worse."

Soothed by Norah's ministrations, Hilda sat quietly, her feet wriggling gratefully in the cool grass. The darkness was welcome; her eyes always recoiled from the light when her head was bad. But the cicadas—would they never stop? That incessant buzz . . .

"Norah, I am sick in my stomach," she said suddenly, then moaned and bent over, retching.

The next few minutes were nasty, but Norah was kind, and when the spasms had worn themselves out and Norah had wiped the sufferer's mouth and scuffed dust over the remains of her supper, Hilda felt a good deal better. The pain would linger for a time, she knew, but the worst was over.

"It's your eyes, maybe," Norah offered. "You should see a doctor. You're havin' these spells more often, seems like."

Hilda leaned back against a tree and yawned, her need for sleep almost overpowering now that the severest pain had receded. "It is not my eyes, I think. It is the heat, and the work, and the worry about your brother and the rest. I cannot talk about it now, I am too tired, but there are things I must do. John Bolton knows something about that terrible man who shot the president. I am sure of it now, but I cannot make him tell. Yet."

Norah sighed. "I'm tryin' not to think about it, but when I see my brother . . ."

"Tomorrow is Sunday. We will see our families, and I will see Patrick and learn what he knows. You will tell me what you learn?"

"If he'll talk about it. And you'll tell me?"

Hilda nodded and yawned again. "I am sorry, Norah. It is not that I do not care, but I must sleep."

"I know. Don't worry yourself. The day's been long enough for the troubles it's held. We'll look at it all again in the mornin'."

Arm in arm, the two girls slipped back into the house, not forgetting to put the chain on the door.

5

A party of eight, representing the Chicago Automobile club, passed through South Bend [on Sunday, September 8] at 12 o'clock, enroute to Buffalo, N. Y.
—South Bend *Tribune*, September 9, 1901

A SPRINKLE began a few minutes after Hilda went to bed. She lay listening to the thud of huge raindrops against the window, waiting for the coolness that would surely come, but the sound stopped after a few minutes, to be replaced by a rising, though still hot, wind and the distant rumble of thunder. She turned restlessly in her narrow bed. The dull ache in her head, releasing its hold only slowly, grudgingly, robbed her of the sleep she needed so badly. Once she rose and went to the window, praying for real rain. By the occasional flare of lightning, brighter now, she could see, far below her on the drive, that the brief drizzle had been licked up by the thirsty dust near the carriage house. There hadn't been enough rain even to create a mud puddle.

It was an hour or more before the real rain came, suddenly, with a brilliant flash of lightning and a doom crack of thunder and a rush of cool, sweet-smelling air. The curtains would get wet; so would the floor. Utterly indifferent to these domestic disasters and to the noise of the storm, Hilda turned over, pulled up the coverlet, and slept.

She slept as one drugged, drugged with the blessed relief from pain, and woke refreshed and full of vigor. The rain still pattered on the roof. Hilda was not discouraged. It was Sunday, the day was her own, and . . .

"Norah, it is cool!" She burst into Norah's bedroom next door with the joyful news. "I can breathe again!"

"Mmph." The sound came from somewhere in the mound of bedclothes.

Sundays at Tippecanoe Place were made as easy as possible for the servants, who were expected to go to church, but were then free for the day. The family always breakfasted buffet style on Sundays, so Norah was excused from her waitress duties and needed to help only with clearing away. This morning she was taking full advantage of the extra time to sleep. She could always slip into the latest mass.

"We must talk, Norah. We must plan what we will do, what you will say to your brother."

An arm reached out. A pillow was pulled over a tousled dark head.

"Norah!"

The mound rose and fell, gently, rhythmically.

Hilda gave it up. There were things she needed to discuss with Norah, but perhaps it would be better to find out what she could before that discussion. There was no doubt that she and Norah were going to have to tread very cautiously in any encounter with Flynn and his dubious friends; best, maybe, to know in what direction they needed to go.

Hilda was not quite the heedless adventuress she had been a year before when she had become involved in a murder investigation, but she still enjoyed the idea of herself as crusader. Nursing a noble but somewhat confused self-image, a mixture of the Norse gods, St. George, and Joan of Arc, Hilda went down to breakfast, head held regally high.

"Thinkin' well of yerself this mornin', are ye?"

"Good morning, Mrs. Sullivan." Hilda inclined her head graciously. Her braids were shining and golden, and pinned to her head in perfect order. "I am feeling very well, thank you. The breakfast smells very good," she added, the queen condescending to her subjects.

Mrs. Sullivan rolled her eyes.

Hilda ate breakfast with enthusiasm (having lost most of her evening meal), hurried through the few chores that fell to her lot of a Sunday, and dressed carefully for church, St. George donning armor for the battle. The almost new blue-wool skirt Mrs. George had given her, she decided, was very becoming and appropriate for a chilly day, and her freshly laundered white waist with the lace insertions, also a gift from her employer, would look nice with it. The old black felt hat would have to do—it was too late for the summer straw—but Hilda recklessly pulled one of the blue feathers from the straw hat, pinned it to the band of the despised black felt, and secured the construction to her head with a slightly bent hat pin, six inches long, that would have served as a handy dagger in any sort of fight.

A crocheted shawl around her shoulders, Hilda sailed forth.

It was going to be a fine day. The rain had nearly stopped, and the birds, cheered by relief from the long dry spell, sang with springlike abandon. A brisk wind sent clouds flying across the sky. Leaves, still green but with their bonds to the trees already autumn-weakened, had been blown down in copious quantities. They lay thickly underfoot, wet and slippery; Hilda had to step carefully. And when the sidewalk ended and the mud began, she had to lift her skirts. It would never do to arrive at church with a muddy hem. As it was, when Hilda joined her brother and sisters at the door of the tiny church, Gudrun clucked over the state of her sister's boots and insisted she clean them before they all went inside.

The congregation was unusually solemn that morning, and the prayers for the president very fervent. Even the conversation afterward, on the church lawn, was subdued. As was his habit, Olaf Lindahl sought out Hilda, and as was her habit, Hilda turned away from him to talk with his sister Ingrid—a boring sort of girl, but at least she didn't make sheep's eyes at Hilda the way her brother did.

"Good day, Ingrid," she said in Swedish. "I hope you are well?"

She didn't look well, Hilda observed. There were dark circles under her eyes, and her mouth looked pinched.

"I am tired," replied Ingrid. "I do not know how you can look so fresh. But perhaps you do not work as hard as I do."

"I work very hard!" Hilda retorted. "These past few days—"

"But there are many servants at Tippecanoe Place, and your master and mistress, they are kind," Ingrid went on in a whine. "At the Warren house there is only me and the gardener, and Mr. Warren, he scolds all the time, he says the work is not well done. But Mrs. Warren, she does not know how to manage a household, and there should be more servants. I cannot do it all myself."

Well, Hilda had heard it all before, and knew the Warrens almost as well as Ingrid did. She gritted her teeth and listened, instead, to the birdsong until she was rescued by Gudrun.

"It is time for dinner, sister. Come."

Perhaps by way of reaction to the solemnity of the church service, when the family had walked to the tiny, snug "factory house" where all except Hilda lived, her younger sister was even more talkative than usual.

"Have you heard about the excitement, Hilda?" Freya was bursting with news that she had not been allowed to impart until the solemn part of Sunday was over.

"What excitement?"

"The automobiles!"

Sven frowned, but Freya ignored him.

"Bjorn Linberg told me. A group of automobiles will try to travel all the way from Chicago to Buffalo, and this morning some of them passed through South Bend!"

"Hmph!" said Gudrun. "A fine way to spend a Sunday morning, I do not think!"

"But it is exciting! They are gasoline machines, and one of them"—Freya giggled—"one of them stopped at a gasoline repository for more fuel, and took the door of the building off its hinges, and had to return to Chicago!"

Hilda laughed at that, too, but Gudrun drew her brows together. "Such foolishness! Not fit for a Sunday."

Sven nodded his agreement and they dropped the subject. It didn't do to upset Gudrun while she was putting the final touches on the meal. She was an excellent cook, and Sunday dinner was her weekly tour de force: salt herring with sour cream; roast pork; beets pickled with sugar and vinegar; lacy potato pancakes with onions; tart, tangy soup made with dried fruits; wonderful crisp flat bread; hot, strong coffee. Hilda ate her way solidly through the feast, her appetite unimpaired by her hearty breakfast, while thinking nostalgically about her mother and younger siblings, still back in Sweden.

"I wonder what they will eat for Sunday dinner?" she said in the Swedish that they always used in the family.

"Have eaten, my little chick," corrected Sven, knowing at once what she was talking about. "It is evening there now."

"Oh, I know." Hilda wriggled a little in her chair, a carved and painted one Sven had made himself. "I do not like to think about it. It makes them seem so far away."

"They will not have had a dinner so good as this," said Gudrun a little sadly. "Mamma is a good cook, better than I, but they are not rich, as we are."

It was a gross understatement. The tiny farm near the tiny village of Björka had barely provided a living for their large family even when their father had been alive. After he died, their mother and the older children were hard put to grow enough in the rocky ground to feed themselves. And when representatives of the Studebakers had come to Sweden to recruit factory workers and Sven had decided to chance it, the three eldest girls, with the daring born of desperation, had come to America with him to try to earn money.

They had all succeeded. Sven, with his woodworking skills, had worked his way up to a responsible job in the body shop, assembling wagon beds and carriage bodies and sometimes carving details for the fanciest models. Hilda, the prettiest of the girls, had found little trouble in getting her housemaid job, a position in which appearance was nearly as important as skill. Gudrun and Freya both worked in wealthy, respectable houses, and the four of them, if not precisely rich, earned enough that they could eat well even while sending frequent gifts home to Sweden and saving money to bring the rest of the family here.

"Five years we have been here now, or almost," said Freya with a sigh.

"But we have nearly enough money." Sven smiled at them. "We must not be gloomy, my sisters, even on such a dreary day. We have gone to our church, we have eaten a meal fit for the Studebakers themselves, and soon Mamma and Elsa and Birgit and Erick will be with us."

"And they had good coffee today, anyway, and some dessert," said Gudrun. "I sent them ten pounds last month, and some dried apples and apricots; they should have the package by now."

"And this is a good time for fish from the lake," Sven went on, "and there was a pig ready to slaughter as soon as the weather was cold. You remember, Mamma told us in her last letter. So you see, little chick, you must not worry."

But Hilda sighed. "It is not only about them that I worry." Her self-assured mood of the morning had fallen away. There were some questions she must ask Sven, but she must go carefully. "There is the president, and the anarchists. It is a terrible thing."

Gudrun clucked and shook her head. "You are right, Hilda. It is a terrible thing that in America we can have these anarchists, that they can plot to kill the president—"

"I have heard," said Freya, interrupting, "that it was not a plot, that it was all the one man's doing, the man who shot him—"

"Nonsense!" Gudrun frowned at her. "The police hunt for anarchists all over the country, to put them in prison where they belong."

"Are they—do you think they will look for them here?"

Sven had just gotten his after-dinner pipe going nicely. He removed it from his mouth and looked up sharply at Hilda's question. "And why should they look for them here?"

"It is only—oh, I do not know. But there is trouble with laboring men everywhere, strikes in Pittsburgh and Chicago and —I only thought that, with much industry here in South Bend, there might be some unrest. Is there—do you know if the men talk at Studebaker's about problems, about . . ."

She stopped talking. Sven was looking at her with a severity she had never seen before. He pointed the stem of his pipe at her, jabbing the air with emphasis as he spoke.

"There is no trouble at the Studebaker factory. Do you understand me? None! I will not allow you to make such remarks. Guard your tongue well, Hilda. You must never suggest such a thing again!"

As his sisters stared in astonishment, he stalked out of the room and stamped up the stairs to his bedroom.

6

What is that which the breeze, o'er the towering steep,
As it fitfully blows, half conceals, half discloses?
— Francis Scott Key, "The Star-Spangled Banner," 1814

HILDA left as soon as she decently could, much disturbed in mind and more than a little hurt. Never before had Sven shouted at her. Never! He took his role as elder brother seriously, and had often reproved her, but gently, kindly. Why was he now so upset?

She scowled at the leaves underfoot and stepped up her pace.

"Good afternoon, Miss Johansson."

She looked up, startled. Flynn Murphy stood in front of her, cap in hand and an impudent grin adorning his face. His abundant black hair sprang up in a rampant cowlick.

"And is it a frown I see below those beautiful golden tresses? On such a lovely face, too, if you'll pardon the familiarity!"

She scowled more fiercely. "I will frown if I like, Mr. Murphy, and my face is none of your concern. And you, I do not know that you have any reason to be overpleased with life today."

Flynn held up his hands, the picture of injured innocence. "And why would you be sayin' that?"

Hilda clucked with irritation. "Your sister, she worries about you. She says that you have done bad things, foolish things, and that you will get into trouble. You should be ashamed to worry her so."

"Now, Miss Johansson, you mustn't take everything our Norah says so serious. She's a darlin' girl, an' well I know it, but she's just like me mum—she worries too much. I've done nothin' I've any cause to regret, and I'll be in no trouble."

"What *have* you done, then? Have you met this terrible man, this assassin?" Hilda didn't know why she asked that; Flynn certainly wouldn't tell her.

The grin wavered for a moment. Or maybe it was the flicker of sunlight, glinting briefly through the clouds. "Now, there's a fine subject for a Sunday afternoon—I don't think. Look there at that patch of blue sky. It's goin' to be a fine day, and we stand here scarin' ourselves about assassins! Would you like me to walk you home, Miss Johansson? So nobody jumps out at you? It's more than happy I'd be to walk with such a beautiful girl as you."

"Oh, go about your business!"

"I'm at your command!" He gave her a saucy salute and strolled away. Hilda stood looking after him, shaking her head. A naughty little boy was what he was, cocky as any young male in the barnyard. But she couldn't help liking him. No one could dislike Flynn—though she understood why Norah fretted.

Exasperated with Flynn and worried about Sven, Hilda was not in a sunny mood as she walked up the drive to Tippecanoe Place, and she wasn't pleased to encounter John Bolton near the back door. "Good day, John," she muttered, and turned to go into the house.

"Hmph. Going in with your boots in that state, are you? His Almightiness'll have something to say about that."

"The state of my boots is nothing to do with you."

"Oh, no? You've complained about mine, often enough, you and the rest of them."

"Yours, they smell of the stables. This is only mud."

"And is it my fault I've a dirtier job than yours? And for less pay, too?" His voice was rising. "If there were any justice in the world, I'd be paid more than you. But then, I don't have a pretty face to please the master of the house. Master! Slave master, or near enough!"

"John Bolton, you will not talk that way about Mr. Clem!" Hilda kept her voice to a furious whisper. "What is the matter with you, that you talk so crazy? This is not a good time for talk like that, and it is not true, anyway!" She whirled and ran down the back steps to the kitchen entrance.

Patrick, who had come to pay his usual Sunday afternoon call, was waiting for her in the servants' room.

"You look cold, me girl. Come in the kitchen and sit by the stove for a warm. I've somethin' to tell you—"

"Patrick, you will not give me orders! I must go and clean my boots."

She dropped her shawl on a chair with a fine gesture and swept upstairs. Mrs. Sullivan, who had been catnapping in her favorite rocking chair, looked at Patrick and shrugged.

"In one of her moods. She'll likely need some sweet talk."

"Oh, I can do that! I can talk as sweet as ye please."

"That you can. It's the fine Irish tongue you've got."

"Not," said Patrick with a sigh, "that it does me much good around Hilda."

Hilda returned shortly, still in no mood for blarney.

"Ah, and it's fine you're lookin' today, the roses in your cheeks, the sparkle in your eye—"

"My cheeks are red because I was cold, and if my eyes sparkle it is because I am angry. You said you had something to tell me. If it is nothing more important than the way I look, be silent or go away." She sat in one of the straight chairs around the table and tapped her foot.

Stung, Patrick folded his arms across his chest. "Ah, well, it's only the biggest news in town, but if you don't want to hear it, I know how to keep me mouth shut."

They glared at each other, two strong wills, each daring the other to give in. In the end it was Patrick who capitulated; it almost always was.

"Hilda, truly, it's important."

"Then tell it. And sit. I do not like to look up at you."

Patrick sat, with a glance at Mrs. Sullivan, who had dropped back into her doze. He lowered his voice.

"It's murder, Hilda!"

"Who? When?" Her pique was instantly forgotten. She stared at him, eyes wide, and he was quick to continue.

"They don't know when, for sure. They found the bodies—"

"*Bodies?* More than one?"

Patrick nodded. "Two men. They found 'em this afternoon, at the new city hall."

Hilda frowned. "But why would anyone be there? It is a mere pile of stones; they have only begun to build—"

"Yes, and it was the contractor who was killed!"

"Patrick! But that is Mr. Warren! I know him! He comes here for dinner sometimes, and Ingrid works at his house—it is—I cannot—I did not like him, but—" She stopped and took a deep breath. Mrs. Sullivan stirred; Hilda glanced at her and continued in a lower tone. "You said two . . ."

He nodded again. "The other was one of the workmen, they think. They're not sure yet of his name, or they weren't, the last I heard. But, Hilda, you haven't heard the most peculiar thing! The one man, Mr. Warren, was all wrapped up in the flag!"

"Flag? I do not understand."

"The Stars and Stripes! He was covered with an American flag!"

That shocked Hilda nearly as much as the murders themselves. Though proud of her Swedish heritage, she was an enthusiastic patriot, eager to become an American citizen as soon as possible. The flag of her adopted country was a sacred symbol, and its use as a shroud for a murdered man was deeply disturbing.

"But why, Patrick? For why would they do such a terrible t'ing?"

He shrugged. "Nobody knows. Nobody knows much of anything yet."

"Tell me all you know," she demanded urgently.

Patrick obliged. The bodies, it seemed, had been discovered shortly after noon by a churchgoer walking home along North Main Street. He had stopped to look at the progress of the new building and had seen, through an opening left for an eventual

window, the odd shape of the flag, lying on the ground and billowing in the gusty wind.

"And he didn't think that was right, what with the mud and
all, so he climbed over a low spot in a wall, and that's when he
saw the other man's body—they were lyin' a few feet apart."

Hilda shivered, remembering her own discovery, over a year
before, of a faceless body. It was not a memory she cared to
dwell on. "How were they killed, Patrick?"

"Don't know. The man went to the police, o' course, and
they came and found the other body under the flag. One of 'em
recognized Mr. Warren. Well, he's an important man in
town—"

"So was the other man important, Patrick! The workers, the
poor people, they are just as important—"

"Yes, yes," said Patrick hastily, recognizing one of Hilda's
hobbyhorses, one that she would ride for some time if not instantly distracted. "I didn't mean to say he wasn't, only that
none o' the police knew his face straight off. They're out now,
tryin' to find out who he might be."

"If they do not know who he is, how do they know he was a
workman?" asked Hilda with ruthless logic.

"The way he was dressed, I suppose, or just the fact that he
was there at the buildin' site with the boss. I don't know,
meself."

"And they do not know how they died? That does not seem—"

"I said I don't know how they died. I didn't see 'em meself,
mind. Some o' me police friends brought the news to the fire
station, when I was there talkin' to the lads, but it was after the
bodies were taken away, so all I've got is hearsay. I've heard they
were shot. Then there's the tale they were stabbed, an' the one
as says they were hit over the head. Likely by now there's one
says they were shot full of arrows by red Indians. You know how
rumors fly when somethin' bad happens."

Oh, yes, Hilda knew the force of rumor and innuendo. That
terrible tide had nearly caused the lynching of a Chinese man
last year, for no reason at all save rumor, fear, and the hatred of
so very foreign a foreigner.

Foreigners. Hatred. Hilda looked at the snoring Mrs. Sullivan and lowered her voice almost to a whisper. "Patrick," she said, staring at him intently, "did anyone say anything about —about anarchists?"

"About who?"

His brows knit in simple puzzlement, and Hilda felt almost giddy with the wave of relief that washed over her. She was embarrassed to admit, even to herself, how worried she had been about Patrick, but he plainly had no guilty secrets. And anyway, she had no business to be so concerned about someone who was simply a friend. Had she?

She stood up and adopted a brisk tone to conceal her confused feelings. "Come, Patrick, I wish to talk to you, and I cannot speak always in whispers. There are chairs in the kitchen."

The kitchen, which last night had been a torture chamber of heat, was on this chilly afternoon a pleasantly cozy retreat. Supper would be cold, or else the hastily reheated leftovers of last night's neglected meal, so the fire in the big range was banked down to a comfortable warmth. Hilda filled a blue enamel pot with water and ground coffee and put it on the gas plate, a new innovation feared and despised by Mrs. Sullivan, but handy, in Hilda's opinion, for a quick bit of cooking when the range wasn't up to temperature.

"Now," said Patrick when she had sat down on a wooden kitchen chair and he had pulled another up next to her. "What in the name of all the saints put anarchists into your head?"

"It is because of Czolgosz, the assassin."

"That isn't the way to pronounce it," Patrick interrupted. "I asked Lefkowicz. You remember him, the patrolman? He says it's—well, I can't say it the way he did, but something like Chol-gozh."

"Yes." Hilda waved her hand impatiently. "However you say his name, did you know he was in South Bend only a few weeks ago?" Convinced by now that this was documented fact, Hilda watched eagerly for Patrick's reaction to the startling news.

"I don't believe it," said Patrick flatly. "What made you come up with a harebrained idea like that?"

"Patrick! It is true! The newspaper said so!"

"Which newspaper was that?"

"The *Tribune*, yesterday. I will find it for you, I—"

"Don't bother, me girl. I read it meself—the bit about him bein' from Cleveland, and them talkin' to his stepmother, an' all?"

"Yes, Patrick, and it *said*—"

"All it said was that he'd been in Indiana. It didn't say where."

Hilda blinked. Now that she thought about it, the newspaper account *had* said something like that. Then why was she so certain . . . oh, yes!

"And what would you say, Patrick Cavanaugh, if I told you I knew someone who'd seen and talked with him here?"

7

It is high time that the American people dealt with the anarchist in a way that he deserves. That is, put him under guard or make him leave the country.
—editorial, South Bend *Tribune*, September 7, 1901

AND who might that be?" His tone was doubtful in the extreme.

"John Bolton."

Patrick's eyes narrowed. John was not one of his favorite people. He was English, for a start, and like all the English, inclined to sneer at Irishmen. And Patrick didn't trust John's intentions toward Hilda any more than Hilda herself did. But he had not, up until now, considered John to be much more than a nuisance—not, certainly, a menace to society.

"What did he tell you?" he asked at last, and his voice was sharp.

"It is what he did not tell me," she replied, and proceeded to relate the conversation.

"It is not much, I agree, Patrick," she said when she had finished. "You will say I know nothing. But you were not there; you did not see his face, or the way he handled the horses, or—oh, I cannot tell you every reason why I know, but I do know. I am sure. That man was here in this city, and John knows all about it!"

Her voice had risen with her passion, and Patrick patted her hand. "Hush, darlin' girl. You don't have to argue wi' me. I believe you. I don't say I'd've thought it of Bolton, though the man's a rogue of an English bas—an Englishman." He hoped Hilda's English wasn't good enough to supply the word he had bitten off in the middle. "But what makes you think anarchists had anything to do with the murders here?"

Hilda had not stopped to analyze what was merely a strong intuition. She did so now, slowly counting off ideas on her fingers.

"The city hall is a gift from Mr. Oliver to the city, ja?"

"Ja. Drat it, I mean yes. At least, in a way. South Bend couldn't afford to build new city offices, an' they're needed bad, so Mr. Oliver offered to put up the buildin' for them, and charge only a small rent. So it isn't free, exactly, but it's a fine thing he's doin' all the same."

"And the hall will be used for government business, for—for tax collectors and others. . . ." Hilda was a trifle vague about what activities were conducted in a city hall.

"Yes, and the police department will be there, and assessors, and the issuers of licenses, and . . . the like," said Patrick, who was only a little better informed.

"So. If there were trouble about this new city hall, trouble with the construction, or maybe a scandal, it would hurt Mr. Oliver and it would hurt the city. Mr. Oliver is a rich man, one of the richest men in the city, like the Studebakers. And the city—well, it is the city, the government. Anarchists, they do not like rich men and they do not like the government."

Hilda rose to pour the coffee, restless with her need to express her nebulous ideas. The connections were perfectly clear in her head, but she was having trouble finding the right words in English. She handed Patrick a cup of the rich, fragrant brew and took a sip herself, hoping its strength would clear her mind.

Finally she shook her head and spoke, low and urgently. "Patrick, I cannot say it well. But in my mind I know there is something bad in this city. Something—hard, and ugly, and dangerous. Anarchists, I think maybe, but maybe I am wrong and it is yoost—just—angry men, men who are full of hate. It is, anyway, in this town and—and Patrick, in this house. John Bolton, he has brought it here."

Her coffee cup rattled in its saucer. She set it on the table carefully and clasped her hands. "Patrick, I am afraid."

"And you're right to be, if it's the way you think," said Patrick.

Hilda was startled. She had hoped to be soothed and comforted. Patrick's words provided no comfort, and his next were even more surprising.

"So what are you goin' to do about it?"

She took a deep breath, and when she spoke, she was fully in command of herself again. "I—Patrick, you do not tell me to do nothing, to let someone else, the men, worry about it? You do not tell me I am a weak woman and must—must clean and dust only?"

"And would it do any good if I did?"

"Oh. No, I do not think so." Hilda smiled a little. "But you have before told me such things."

"Yes, and I've learned me lesson, darlin' girl. I've not got so much breath in me as to waste it sayin' things you'll not listen to. You're goin' to try to find out who killed those two men, aren't you?"

"I . . . yes." Hilda had expected, and prepared for, an argument. She felt as though she had stepped on a stair that wasn't there. There was, it seemed, no need to justify her actions, but she went on doing so anyway. "I want to know, Patrick. I do not like it that bad things happen here, here in my city. And I do not think the police here do always a good yob—job—when there are questions about a death. You know that they sometimes choose the answer they like best, rather than look for the truth."

"Are you tryin' to convince yourself, then?" Patrick's tone was rich with irony, and Hilda's dimples showed again for a moment.

"Maybe that is what I do. But, Patrick, you will help me, *ja*?"

"Mmm," he temporized. "What help d'you want?" When Hilda was launched on a project, he had learned, caution was always wise.

"Oh, do not worry! I do not ask you to put yourself in danger! I will face the danger if it is needful."

"Hah! Think yourself fine and brave, don't you? And who was so afraid just a minute ago, I ask you that?"

"I *am* brave," she retorted, stung. "I was only—it was only—I wished to know what you—oh, do not mind that now!" She stamped her foot. "You have more chance than me to talk with people. You know, maybe, more than I do about Mr. Warren. Tell me."

Patrick grinned, pleased to have gotten a rise out of her, and leaned his chair back against the wall. "Well, let's see now. I don't know a lot, mind. He wasn't the sort who'd know somebody like me. But yes, I know some of his men. They say he's—he was—what they call a self-made man. A laborer himself till he piled up a little money and started his own business. That was maybe ten years ago, and since then he'd got rich. Not rich like the Studebakers or the Olivers, but rich enough. Still a Democrat, though, to give the devil his due."

"The devil?" Hilda pounced on the word. "Patrick, you should not use such language, but you did not like him either?"

"Didn't know him, I tell ye. His men didn't like him much."

"Neither did his wife like him, I think. He was rude to her sometimes, and she almost never talked to him when they visited here. She would talk *about* him, making herself important, but I think maybe she was afraid of him. But his men—he was one of them, a laborer like themselves. Why . . . ?"

"That's why. He wasn't a favorite even back in his toilin' days, I hear, but they thought he'd got above himself lately, tryin' to shake the workin' dust off his feet an' forget he was ever a common worker. Drove his men hard, accordin' to the ones I talked to, an' a skinflint when it came to wages."

"Why, then, did they work for him? A good worker can get a good wage here in South Bend."

"He wasn't a good man to cross, from what I hear. If he took against you, he'd not give you a good reference, and you'd find it hard to get any job at all. I know one man, a friend o' mine, said once that Warren was a—a hard man," he improvised rapidly, remembering what his friend had really called the builder. "A hard man, and a secretive one."

"Secretive!" Hilda sounded excited. "What secrets did he hide?"

"Don't know. Me friend didn't know—just said Warren was closemouthed. Didn't like a person to stand too close when he was talkin' business to another man, that sort o' thing. He knew his work, me friend said, an' he was likely honest enough in his business dealin's, but a man who kept his own counsel and didn't trust nobody much."

"But secrets . . ." Hilda looked at Patrick thoughtfully and then shook her head, hard. "We do not know enough."

"Huh! We don't know nothin' at all, me girl."

"We must learn."

"Are you thinkin' of goin' to the police, then?"

"Of course not! They will not talk to me. No, we must speak to our friends, and learn what the people think who are not rich, the unimportant people, what they know."

"Oh, you make out it'll be easy! It won't be, you know. People are scared, or if they aren't now, they will be when the news gets out. They won't want to talk."

"Patrick, you do not think! They will not talk to the police. Of the police they are already frightened, because of the terrible thing that has happened to the president. But they will talk to us; we are just like them."

"I don't know about that." Patrick sounded worried. "There's somethin' . . . now, I don't want you to go gettin' ideas about— well, about nothin' foolish. But me friends at Studebaker's —see, they don't talk to me much these days."

Hilda, with a sudden chill, remembered Sven's strange reaction to her earlier questions. "What do you mean, Patrick? Will not talk to you about what?"

"That's it, you see. We'll be talkin' along, about this and that, and all of a sudden they—dry up, like. Just stop talkin' at all, at all. It's nothin' I can put me finger on, but it's been worryin' me."

Hilda stood up and carefully poured herself a second cup of coffee. She sipped at it, letting the warmth restore her before she dared say more. When she did speak, it was in a frightened whisper.

"Patrick. Today Sven—he would not talk to me. I asked him about the Studebaker works, and he—he became angry with me. Sven! Never, never does he become angry. Stern, sometimes, but not . . ." She swallowed hard and looked at Patrick. "What is it, Patrick? What do these men do, that they will not tell us?"

She sat down and put her coffee cup on the table. Her hands were trembling. They looked at each other, each unwilling to voice what hung in the air between them.

"I'll tell you what I don't like, me girl," said Patrick at last. "I don't like that flag."

"I do not like it either. It is wicked, to use the flag that way. But, Patrick, what is it to do with—"

"I'm gettin' to that. I've been thinkin', you see, *why* was it there?"

"To hide the body, maybe, *ja*?"

"No. If it was that, the killer'd have hid both of the dead men, not just one. No, he had a reason for it. He was tryin' to leave a message."

"What message?"

"I don't know. See, it don't make good sense. They drape heroes' bodies in the flag, soldiers an' that. But the killer wouldn't be tryin' to say Warren was a hero, would he now?"

"N-no." Hilda frowned in thought. "No, but listen, Patrick. If he was an anarchist, he might try to show that this is what happens to patriotic men. It would be very wicked, but . . ."

"Maybe. But Warren wasn't known for bein' patriotic, that I know of. It isn't like he was a veteran, or even a politician. No, there's some other reason for that flag, and I've a notion it's goin' to make trouble for all of us!"

"Oh, Patrick, do not say that!" It came out as a wail. Hilda's chin quivered and, despite her best efforts, a tear slid slowly down her cheek.

8

It makes little difference whether this gang was immediately associated with the attempted assassination of one of the noblest of men . . .
—South Bend *Tribune*, September 7, 1901

PATRICK sat in silence for a moment, considering. Then he looked at Hilda and said, "It's Sven you're worried about, isn't it?"

She nodded wordlessly, looking at her lap.

"Well, then, if you don't mind me sayin' so, it's the fool you're bein' an' no mistake!"

That roused her. She turned a furious face up to him. "Patrick Cavanaugh, you will not dare to call me a fool! You should be ashamed, when I am so worried and afraid, to call me bad names! I will not listen to this, I will go and talk to Norah, I will—"

She stood and turned to the door, but he put out a restraining hand.

"Don't be goin' an' losin' your temper, now! I wanted to get some gumption back into you, and I did. You're actin' much more like yourself."

He grinned at her.

"You—you said that to make me—you—" she spluttered.

"Indeed and indeed. An' it worked, didn't it? Now sit back down and hear me out."

"The chair is hard. I prefer to stand."

"Fine, stand then, but don't go runnin' away upstairs till ye've listened to what I have to say."

He leaned against the warm stove, crossed one foot over the other, and hooked his thumbs around his suspenders. Hilda thought he looked very much at home; the thought annoyed her. She stood very straight, her arms crossed, and glared at him.

"There's no need to be lookin' at me that way," he said, undisturbed. "What I'm sayin' is for your own good. And it's just this. Sven Johansson is one o' the best men they've got at Studebaker's. Everybody knows that. He works hard, he's honest and upright, an' nobody can touch him when it comes to workin' with wood. Your brother's got a reputation in this town, girl!"

"I know that! I do not need you to tell me that!"

"Then why in the name o' common sense, girl, are you thinkin' that he might be mixed up in somethin' shady, will you tell me that? I agree there's somethin' funny goin' on at the factory, but I'd bet my last dollar Sven's got nothing' to do with it, an' you ought to be ashamed o' yourself for even thinkin' he has!"

Hilda was not accustomed to being scolded by Patrick; it was usually the other way around. She set her lips tightly together and said nothing.

Patrick continued relentlessly. "You've got a good brain, Hilda. Better than mine, you've told me often enough, and I'll admit it, and handsome of me it is, too!"

Hilda's lips twitched.

"So what I say is, it's time you used it. You'll pardon me sayin' so, but you've been actin' like a—a glass o' jelly that's not been cooked long enough, all wobbly an' meltin' at the edges."

She turned her head aside lest he see her trying not to smile.

"So do some thinkin' with that mind o' yours, and we'll think out what to do. For it's plain enough we must do somethin', but we've got to be smart about it, for there's pitfalls out there, there's no denyin'. Now are you ready to issue marchin' orders?"

He stood up straight and gave her a mock salute, and, hard as she tried not to, she laughed.

"You are impossible! First you call me a fool and then a glass of jelly! I should turn you out!"

"But you won't, because you need me help. Look, darlin' girl, it's gettin' warm in here, and I don't know if you've noticed, what with all your tantrums an' carryin' on, but the sun's come out. Let's go for a walk an' work out a plan. I'm tired o' this kitchen."

Hilda was glad to get out, too. She fetched her shawl from the servants' room where she had left it and then climbed the back steps briskly, working off her embarrassment over her brief fit of panic.

The crisp air smelled sweet, with the first hint of the sharp dried-leaf scent of autumn and the musky smell of the chrysanthemums that drooped under their burden of rainwater in everyone's front yards. Every now and then a gentle breeze stirred the trees and a little shower would drop from the leaves to their heads.

"The water's spoilin' your hat. Here, cover your head with me coat."

"No, Patrick. My hat is old. It cannot look worse than it does. And you cannot take off your coat on the street!"

"It's a fine hat," Patrick said. "And fine it looks on you!"

Well, that was pure blarney, but Hilda let it pass.

They had walked east, without purposeful direction, but when they found themselves crossing the river on the beautiful Jefferson Street Bridge it seemed natural to rest for a bit in Howard Park, just on the other side. The grass was still too wet to sit on, but they spotted an unoccupied wooden bench, and Patrick gallantly wiped off the seat with his handkerchief.

They sat in silence for a little, watching the St. Joseph River flow by. The river, low for weeks, was high now after last night's storms. It looked slow and placid, but Hilda knew that calm surface hid dangerous currents and a great volume of water, enough to power the many factories just downstream, below the dam, and to generate electricity for streetlighting and the electric street railway. The mighty and beautiful river was the reason for South Bend's existence, and the reason for its name, as well, and Hilda always felt a little awed looking at it.

Patrick, who was not easily awed, sat in concentrated thought for a few minutes, but he grew drowsy. This would never do! He tore his eyes away from the hypnotic roll of the river. "Have you been thinkin' then, darlin'?"

"Do not call me darling. I think, *ja*. But, Patrick, I do not think anything that is of use. My brain, it has shut down, maybe. It is good, as you say, but now . . ." She held out her hands in a gesture of exasperation. "We know nothing, nothing! We must know what is planned at the factory—all the factories, maybe —but if no one will talk to us, how are we to learn?"

"Well, now." Patrick expanded almost visibly. "I've been thinkin', meself. And it seems to me we've got to be clever about this. See, if we go askin' our friends what's goin' on at Studebaker's, we'll get nowhere. People clam up; we already know that. But suppose we ask other kinds o' things?"

"What things?" asked Hilda with more than a touch of skepticism.

"That'd be different for you than for me. Me, I'll be talkin' to men. Your friends are women, other maids and that. I don't know what you talk about. Housework?"

"Oh, Patrick, do not be foolish! Housework is dull. It is what we do all day; we do not talk about it in our time off. We talk about people—our families, our friends, the people we work for. Oh, I know! Mr. and Mrs. Clem are coming home. I could start to talk about that and then about the factory, only a little, and see what they say."

"Yes, and you might be able to get in somethin' about the murders, too. Everyone'll be talkin' about them."

Hilda was dubious. "My friends do not like to talk about murder, Patrick. Not this kind of murder. When it is known what happened, when a man kills another man in a fight, sometimes they will say how awful it was, and if they know anything about the men they will talk about them. But when it is this way and they do not know who or where the murderer might be, they are frightened."

"Well, the men'll be talkin' about it right enough. 'Specially in the taverns. I can go there an' listen."

"And drink." Hilda was not a teetotaler like her employers,

but she didn't altogether approve of the amount Patrick could drink on occasion.

"Yes, but not too much this time. It'll be neither a weddin' nor a wake, girl! I'll need to keep me head about me. An' when the time's right, if the conversation comes around to it, there's somethin' else I'm goin' to do." He paused and looked around to make sure nobody else was within earshot.

"I'm goin' to say a thing or two to make 'em think I might be in favor of a spot o' trouble meself, labor trouble, or worse, an' see who takes me up on it."

Hilda drew in her breath sharply. "But, Patrick! That could put you in great danger!"

"I'm not a coward, whatever you think." Her gibe about doing the dangerous jobs herself had hurt.

"No, I do not think you are. A fireman cannot be a coward. But . . ." Her voice trailed off. There were no legitimate objections. It was a good idea, really. He would learn much more about any conspiracy that might exist by pretending sympathy with it. She sighed. "I do not like it, Patrick. But you are right. It was smart of you to think of it."

They could come up with nothing more, though they discussed it until the sun dropped low in the sky and the air grew too chill to sit. On their way back to Tippecanoe Place, they hurried. Hilda's wrap was not warm, and besides, Mr. Williams was most insistent that all the servants be in by sunset on their day off.

Patrick said good-bye and took himself off, and Hilda was making for the kitchen door when she heard her name called. She turned around.

"Hilda." John Bolton walked across the drive from the carriage house and stood before her, his voice pitched low and urgent. "You've not said anything, have you? About what I said earlier? I didn't mean anything by it, you know that."

"I have said nothing. What you say is of no importance to me." She turned away, but he put a hand on her arm.

"Please! I didn't mean it! I was in a bad mood. I—I had a bit too much to drink last night, and—well . . ."

Hilda shook off his arm and looked at him with astonishment. She had never seen John in a contrite mood. He had been in a hurry to speak to her, too. Inside the carriage house stood one of the broughams, apparently just returned, with the horses still hitched up and snorting their impatience to be free.

She tilted her head to one side. Her eyes narrowed. "Why did you drink too much?"

"I—umm—I was with friends."

His manner confirmed Hilda's growing suspicion. "What friends?" she pressed.

"Just—friends."

"John, you wish me to be silent. I wish some information." She let it hang there, looking him straight in the eye.

"Ah, why should I tell you anything? Go ahead and talk! You don't know anything, anyway."

"I know enough to be dangerous to you, John Bolton. The police, they suspect bad things of all anarchists. If I tell them you have met with the very man who shot the president, you will be in jail before you can get those horses out of harness. And you will lose your job. The Studebakers like you, but they are Republicans, important Republicans. Why, they gave the president his carriage!"

He capitulated. "We can't talk here," he muttered. "It's too close to the house." He gestured to the stone bench.

"I cannot stay long. Be quick; the sun will set soon."

"Do you want that information or don't you?" His tone was surly, but there was no real fight in him.

Hilda did not sit on the bench next to John. He would almost certainly not attempt dalliance, not in his present mood, but the bench was too private; no one from the house could see them there. Caution was never a mistake. She stood in front of him, met his eye, and repeated, "What friends?"

"I—it was a meeting."

"And you met to do what?"

Her voice was steely. John fidgeted. "Only to talk."

She waited.

"Oh, very well! It was the same people who'd met the day he came to town."

"Who came to town?" she asked, knowing the answer.

John would not say the name. "You know who," he replied, his face turned away and his voice surlier than ever.

"Who was there?"

"Four or five men. You don't know them."

"Was Patrick one of them?"

He looked at her and sneered. "You'd like to know, wouldn't you?"

"I will know, or I will go straight to Colonel George!"

"Little snitch! No, he wasn't, if you must know. Ruddy Irishman, thinks himself too good to be seen with honest workingmen. There was me, and Kovacz, and Kapinski, and Sobieski, and—" He stopped abruptly.

"And who else?"

"I don't remember."

Hilda rolled her eyes and waited.

"You won't like it!"

Hilda was already aware of that. She swallowed. "Who else was at the meeting?"

"Flynn Murphy."

She persisted until the whole story came out.

"We're afraid, can't you understand that? We met to try to think out what to do. We've done nothing we shouldn't, but we're tarred with the same brush as that madman! If the police find out about us meeting him . . ."

He didn't have to finish the thought. "They must not know! You were foolish to meet again, John."

"I know it, but it was better than sending 'round a letter that might be seen by the wrong people. We had to be sure everyone was keeping his mouth shut, so I talked to Kapinski and he arranged the meeting."

"How?"

John shrugged. "They all live near here. It's not so far from the rich parts of town to the poor ones, you know."

"Where did you meet?"

John looked down at the grass. "Here."

"Here! Here in the carriage house? John, how could you do such a bad t'ing? Mr. Clem would—would—"

John's anger lashed out. "Mr. Clem isn't home, is he? And we were doing no harm. It's the most private place—the others live with their families. Why shouldn't I have my friends come to call after my work's done?"

"John." Hilda's voice was urgent. "The first meeting, the one with—with the other man." Even she hesitated to let the assassin's name cross her lips. "It was not here, was it?"

Hilda had an imagination, a lively, ungoverned imagination that sometimes led her into trouble. She could imagine old Norse spirits everywhere on a dark night, trolls in trees and tomtes under houses, waiting to work mischief. Now she imagined a meeting of anarchists, their eyes dark and wild, brandishing weapons—knives and even guns—and shouting destruction, exploding from this very stable to wreak havoc throughout the town. . . .

John shook his head. "No. And thank God for that! I'd not like to think . . . no, it was at a tavern on Division Street."

"What did—he—speak about?"

A shrug. "The usual. How the workingman's oppressed, and the government's no good. He'd been going to Emma Goldman's lectures and he was all fired up, but he rambled on and didn't make a lot of sense. It was dead boring, if you want to know." He paused and then went on more slowly. "He did say one odd thing, though. I'd forgotten. He said he'd be a lot better dressed when he went to Buffalo. Or when he came back from Buffalo, I forget. I didn't know what he meant, and I left just after that." John looked at the floor. "Do you think he was talking about . . . ?"

Hilda made no reply.

"Look, there was no harm in it! How was I to know the man was crazy? He was right about some things, you know. The workingman in this country *is* oppressed, and it *is* time something was done about it, but not . . ." Again he ran out of words. "Hilda, you won't tell anybody, will you? There was no harm in it, not really."

There were a dozen things Hilda would have liked to say, to ask, but the sun was sinking lower and lower in the sky.

"I must go! I will talk to you another time, but, John"—she hesitated and her voice softened a little— "do not worry. I will tell no one."

9

Columbus, O.
The Young Men's Christian Association, of this city, yesterday launched a movement for the suppression of anarchy in the United States . . .
　　　　　—South Bend *Tribune*, September 9, 1901

S HE ran to the back steps and pelted down them to the kitchen door, and it was as well she hurried. Mr. Williams was waiting for her, Rex close by his side. Both man and dog looked grave.

"Hilda—"

"I am not late! The sun, it is just there, behind the trees—"

"No, no, never mind that! I have bad news."

Hilda's hand went to her heart. "Not—the president, he is not—"

"The president is resting quietly, according to the latest bulletins. This is family news."

She knew by his tone of voice which family he meant. She looked at him with sudden apprehension.

"Mr. and Mrs. Clem landed in New York today, but Mr. Clem took a serious fall as he disembarked. He was taken to a hotel in a good deal of pain, and we do not now know when he will be able to come home. He may have broken his leg. And he is not a young man, nor in good health. . . ."

Hilda didn't need to hear what the butler left unsaid. Her heart plummeted. If serious trouble was really blowing up at

Studebaker's, what might happen with the captain of the ship unable to take his place at the helm?

When Hilda went up to bed that night, Norah was right behind her.

"Flynn got drunk this afternoon," she said without preamble, once she had seated herself on Hilda's only chair.

Hilda dropped her buttonhook. "But I saw him, when I returned from my family! He was yoost—just—as always, then. I do not know where he had been, but I thought he was going home. Did he instead go to a tavern?"

"No, he was doin' his drinkin' at home, for a change. Mum wouldn't let him go out with that bunch o' toughs he's been hangin' out with, nor she wouldn't let them come to the house. It wasn't decent, she said, not with the president lyin' there between life an' death. But she didn't try to keep him from the beer. Better to drink with his family, if he had to drink at all, she said. An', Hilda, he said a lot o' strange things!"

Hilda retrieved the buttonhook and began again to wiggle a stubborn boot button out of its hole. She must give nothing away; she had promised John. But if she played this carefully, she could keep her promise and still gain useful information. "What things? Bad?"

"I—I don't just know. The rest of us are talkin', see, about the president an' all, an' me brother Kevin, he says he thinks the killin's here are by the same gang of assassins, or else why was the poor man all wrapped up in the flag? An' me mum starts on about what a shame an' a scandal it is, and Flynn, he gets all excited an' says we none of us know a thing about it. None o' the anarchists, he says, would touch the flag on a bet, 'cause they despise it."

"Oh! That is wicked!"

"That's what we all said, an' I thought me mum was goin' to take a slipper to Flynn, for all he's a foot taller than her. But he stops talkin' about that an' starts goin' on about how there's goin' to be big changes in the world, big changes here in this town, he says. Talkin' all excited, like it'd be a new world!"

"And then what did he say?"

"Nothin'," said Norah, her voice flat with anticlimax. "He passed out."

"Did any of your other brothers or sisters know what he meant?"

"Nothin' that made any sense. He likes you; did he say anythin' to you earlier?"

"Only that he will not be in trouble. He is like a little boy, Norah!"

Norah sighed. "He is that, an' most o' the time his pranks are harmless as a boy's. But Hilda, I don't like the sound of this, an' that's the truth!"

She would, Hilda thought, like it even less if she knew about the meetings.

Hilda slept badly. John's involvement with anarchists, Flynn's portents of disaster, and the news of Mr. Clem's accident worked their way into her dreams, dreams of vague terror that she couldn't remember the next morning. The one detail that did linger was the flag, the Stars and Stripes, waving through her troubled sleep. That flag was important; she was sure of it.

As she went about her duties the next morning, snapping at the dailies with unaccustomed bad temper, she could not worry out of her mind any satisfactory explanation for any of it. Too much was happening, too many calamities. What could possibly come next?

What came next, as is sometimes the contrary way of things, was good news. The Western Union boy arrived at noon with a telegram from New York. Mr. Williams took it to Colonel George, gave it to him with hands that trembled, and hesitated in the doorway.

"It's all right, Williams," said Colonel George, a smile breaking out on his face as he read. "Father's feeling much better. He and Mother will stay in New York for a day or two, but they plan to be home on Friday. It's their wedding anniversary, by the way."

"Yes, indeed, sir. Thirty-seven years, if I recall rightly."

Colonel George nodded. "Quite right. You have a good memory."

"Thank you, sir. It's very good news, sir."

And he was off to spread the word to the rest of the servants.

When he got to the servants' room, it was abuzz with more good news, extracted (by means of a large piece of fresh peach shortcake) from the Western Union boy. President McKinley was much improved. The doctors even thought he might pull through! When Mr. Williams made his contribution to the good tidings, the staff rejoiced so loudly he felt obliged to speak sternly to them.

Hilda was, of course, happy that Mr. Clem was feeling better, but she was unable to rejoice with the others. What if he came home to a strike, or even worse labor troubles? It would break his heart, perhaps even his health.

It was important to learn all she could of what might happen. She could do little herself to stave it off, but knowledge was power. She would forgo her afternoon rest and go do some snooping.

With unusual prudence, she asked Mr. Williams's permission instead of sneaking out. "For I wish to tell my sisters about Mr. Clem, sir. They will be so happy. I will return promptly at two o'clock."

It sounded reasonable enough to the butler, who was ready to believe that Mr. Clem's state of health was of immense concern to every resident of the city. "Very well. It is your rest time. If you choose to spend it in this way, you may. See you do come back on time. The house must be in perfect order for Mr. Clem's return."

Well, Hilda knew that, but she was in too much of a hurry to carp at the butler's fussiness. She didn't bother with a hat, but simply left on her maid's cap and sped off to the house down the street, where Freya worked.

The butler there was not overly fond of Hilda, whom he considered to be flighty and a bad influence on Freya. It was fortunate, therefore, that Freya was herself just coming out the door when Hilda arrived.

"Sent on an errand," she explained in Swedish. "I have to match some embroidery silk at Ellsworth's. You can come if you like."

There was nothing Hilda wanted more, so the two turned east up Washington Street. The stately trees that lined the streets seemed to droop in heavy, humid air. It wasn't hot, especially, but Hilda was uncomfortable, her temper close to the surface.

"Aren't you afraid someone will see you?" asked Norah.

"I have permission," Hilda replied shortly.

"Never! From that old troll?"

"I told him I wanted to tell my sisters that Mr. Clem's health is improved, and that he and Mrs. will be home in a few days. He fell yesterday, getting off the boat in New York, but it now seems he was not seriously hurt."

"That is good," said Freya. "Sven has been worried that he was not here."

That was Hilda's cue, and she jumped on it. "Freya, is something wrong at the factory? Sven acted very strange yesterday when I asked."

Freya shook her head in exasperation. "I do not know. He says nothing to us, only one day he said he hoped Mr. Clem would be home soon, that the company needed its president at a time like this. And when we asked what he meant, he would not say any more and told us, Gudrun and me, not to tell anyone what he had said."

Well, that was frustrating, but expected. Hilda judged it best not to pursue that topic any further. She didn't want word to get back to Sven that she was interested.

"Well, I will not tell him you told me. Freya, have you heard about the murders yesterday?"

"Of course I have heard. The bread man talked of nothing else this morning. I suppose you went right down to see the bodies."

"Freya! I do not like to look at bodies! How can you say such a thing?"

"Oh, I just thought—you and murder—"

The look in Hilda's eyes stopped her; she went on in a less frivolous tone. "I suppose Patrick told you all about it. What have you heard?"

"Not very much. Only the name of one of the victims, Mr. Warren, and that he was wrapped in the American flag. That, Freya, that is very bad. That I do not like."

"No, you are right, that was a wicked thing. You did not hear, then, that the other man was one of his workmen?"

"That, yes, but not his name. Patrick said the police did not yet know who he was."

"They know now, but it is a Polish name, and difficult—I do not remember."

Polish, not Irish or Swedish. Hilda breathed a silent prayer of thanks that the victim was not likely to be anyone she knew. "How were they killed, Freya? Patrick did not yet know that, either."

"Oh, so there are sometimes things the famous Patrick does not know!" The look appeared again on Hilda's face. "All right, all right, I will tell you! They were hit on the head, maybe with a piece of wood, or a pipe. Their heads were—" Freya shuddered. "I do not want to talk about it, and I think you do not want to know, but they were badly hurt. There is talk"— here Freya lowered her voice and glanced around her quickly— "there is talk that it was the work of some of the men working on the building, that they did not like Mr. Warren and were about to go on strike, and there was a fight."

"Who says that?" Hilda's voice was sharp and quick.

Freya shrugged. "It was the grocery boy who told me."

"I do not think that is right. For this would have happened in the night, or on Sunday morning. And the people who live there would have heard a fight, and would have gone for the police, who are close by."

"Maybe they did."

"Freya! Use your head. No one knew the bodies were there until nearly noon on Sunday. That is not the answer."

Freya tossed her head and pouted. She might have argued, but they were at the door of Ellsworth's Dry Goods Store. Hilda would dearly have liked to go in and linger over the laces and ribbons and braids. She hesitated at the door.

"*May* we pass?" The two women shouldered their way between the sisters with scant ceremony. The taller one remarked, "These foreigners! All over town, and don't know their place! Something ought to be done."

"Hilda, keep your temper," said Freya softly.

Hilda clenched her fists so tightly her nails dug into her palms. "Because we speak Swedish, they despise us. And I know those women! They are Mrs. Coates and Mrs. Singler. I served them at table only last month, and look—they did not even know who I was."

Freya shrugged. "You are a maid. You are dressed as a maid. What do you expect? Are you coming in?"

Hilda took several deep breaths. "No, I have no money, and I must not be late. I will tell you when Mr. Clem will be home, as soon as I know."

She muttered under her breath all the way home. "We clean for them and cook for them and work in their factories, and they do not even know we are people! We ought to . . ." Her mind slowed down, then. This was the way the men felt. This was dangerous thinking. Better try to forget the slight. Certainly she ought to be used to slights by now, and they were of small importance compared to her real worries.

When she rounded the corner of Taylor Street to get to the back drive, she saw that Kristina, the maid next door, was sweeping the front steps. That was fortunate. Kristina was always ready for a chat, and she might have useful information.

She greeted Hilda with a smile and a glance toward the front windows of the house. "Good day, Hilda. If you wish to talk, we had better go into the backyard. Mr. Parker is in the drawing room and might see us."

Mr. Parker was the butler and had the same opinion of Hilda as the other neighborhood butlers had. Giggling a little, Kristina ran down the porch steps and around the side of the house, and Hilda followed.

"You look angry."

"I am. I was, anyway. But I am nearly late. I wanted only to tell you, before I must go in, that Mr. Clem is in better health and will be home in a few days."

Kristina, living right next door, had of course heard about Mr. Clem's fall. She sighed with relief. "That is good. Everyone has been so worried about him. He is a very important man, Hilda, and South Bend, without him . . ." She didn't finish the unpleasant thought.

"Or just Studebaker's, without him," said Hilda mournfully. "It is not to be thought of. I have wondered, of late, whether the factory runs well when he is not here. He has been away so long . . ." She trailed off artistically, and Kristina did not disappoint her.

"Ah, all is not well at the factory, I think maybe. Some men came to the house a few weeks ago. I do not remember their names, but businessmen, important men, I think. They were talking about Studebaker Brothers, and they sounded very worried. You know my English is not so good, and they were speaking very quietly, but I heard one of them say, 'It could ruin them. It is madness!' "

The two girls had been speaking in Swedish, but she quoted the words in English, and Hilda's eyes grew very wide.

10

Chicago
The 12 anarchists arrested here Saturday were arraigned
this morning to answer to the charges of a conspiracy to as-
sassinate the president.
—South Bend *Times*, September 9, 1901

ILDA worried the rest of the afternoon as she went about
her duties, still onerous with the approach of Mr. and
Mrs. Clem's homecoming. She and Anton were polishing
the great, carved front doors—she the wood, he the bronze
hardware—when the evening newspapers arrived. Hilda
dropped her cloth and ran out to intercept the newsboys. There
might, just possibly, be some small item about Studebaker's,
and if she could read it before Colonel George got his hands on
the papers and did who-knew-what with them . . .

The lead stories, of course, dealt with President McKinley's health,
which continued to improve. The *Tribune* was cautiously opti-
mistic about his prospects. The *Times*, somewhat the more sen-
sational paper, had a headline that said unequivocally "Will Pull
Through."

The right-hand columns of the front page, in both papers,
were full of the local murders. Hilda gave one account a cursory
glance, looked more closely, gave a startled gasp, and thrust the
papers into Anton's hands.

"Take them to Mr. Williams." She ran into the house and
rushed downstairs to find Norah.

Her friend was in the family dining room, setting the table

for two; Colonel and Mrs. George were dining alone for a change. When Hilda blew in, Norah nearly dropped the silver knives.

"What're you doin' down here, girl? The missus'll be home any minute, and she'll need you to ladies-maid her."

"Norah! I have seen the papers! The name of the murdered man, the other man, the workman—it was Lefkowicz!"

"Oh. I heard he was Polish." Norah put the knives down in careful alignment on the snowy damask cloth.

"But do you not remember? That is the name of the policeman, the nice one, the patrolman."

"You mean they've up and murdered a *policeman?* Oh, there'll be the devil to pay for that!"

"No, of course not! The newspaper would have said. No, but, Norah, it must be a relation. It is not a common name. Oh, Norah, I must talk to Patrick!"

"You can't. You've work to do till dinner, and then there's our supper, and after that it'll be dark. Mr. Williams'll never let you out."

"I will not ask."

"Hilda!"

She tossed her head; her heavy gold braids trembled under her cap. "The Yale lock on the back door will make it easy. I will not have to climb out of the kitchen window as I used to do. Norah, do not shake your head at me! Do you want me to help Flynn, or do you not?"

"I don't see how you gallivantin' off to Patrick in the middle of the night is goin' to help Flynn!"

"It will not be the middle of the night."

"An' where d'you plan to find Patrick, may I ask you that? You don't even know where he lives. Or do you?" Her voice was loaded with innuendo that Hilda chose to ignore.

"No, I do not. His family does not like me; I am too Protestant. I have never been asked to visit them. But Patrick—he will be at the firehouse."

"An' if he isn't?"

"Then I will not see him until tomorrow, but tonight, Norah, you must help me."

"Hilda, listen to me." Norah put down the rest of the silverware and leaned over the table for emphasis, her hands gripping the back of a chair. "It's a stupid thing you're proposin' to do! You'll get in bad trouble. You can't go off an' talk to a man alone at night! Even if nothin' happens—an' don't you never forget there's murderers about on the streets, an' anarchists, too, for all we know—but even if you don't get killed, or worse, there's your reputation to think of!"

Norah's voice was urgent and pleading. "You've done yourself enough harm, if you don't mind me sayin' so, spendin' so much time with Patrick as you do. I know there's no real harm in it, but there's few others as would say the same."

"Then they need kinder thoughts. Patrick and I, we do nothing wrong. Why may I not see my friend?" She took a deep breath. "But tonight, no matter what the rules, I must talk to him. If no one knows, there will be no harm. Or, Norah, if you come with me . . ."

"Oh, no!" Norah backed away. "Once I went out with you at night, and we near burned down the whole town! No, I'd do almost anythin' for you, you know that, but this I'll not do."

A latch clicked. "Hilda!" Mr. Williams stood in the door of the adjoining butler's pantry. "You have no business to be here! Go upstairs at once; Mrs. George wants you."

Hilda fled, but the two girls continued the argument for the rest of the evening whenever they could snatch odd moments of private conversation. By bedtime neither had budged an inch. Hilda was determined that she would go out, Norah accompanying her; Norah was determined that neither would go anywhere.

"You cannot stop me, Norah," said Hilda defiantly. "I will go alone if I must, but I will go."

"All right, then! Go if you have to! It's a daft thing to do, an' you'll be sorry for it, but go, and stop talkin' about it. You make me tired!"

Hilda took a deep breath and reined in her temper. "Norah.
I will tell you something I promised not to tell."

Norah looked at her suspiciously.

"You will not tell anyone?"

"That depends. If it's anything interestin' . . ."

"It is about Flynn, Norah, and it is very serious."

Now she had her friend's undivided attention.

"I made John Bolton tell me what he knows, and it is all true,
Norah. Leon Czolgosz was in South Bend, and he did hold a
meeting, and—and, Norah, John and Flynn were both there."

"Holy Mother of God!" Norah said in a whisper, making the
sign of the cross.

"I did not mean to tell you, but now you will understand why
I must learn as much as I can, as soon as I can. You must not tell
anyone!"

"No." It was still a whisper.

"So I go now. If anything goes wrong, and I become locked
out of the house, I will throw gravel at your window. You will
come down then and let me in?"

"Yes."

Hilda looked at her doubtfully. "I am sorry to worry you,
Norah. It is for the best. I will be away for only a little time."

The household had settled down early that night, and Hilda
wished she could do the same. She was weary from hard work
and worry, and she had not had her usual rest, but she turned
away from her tempting bed. Draping a cloak over her black uniform, she crept down the back stairs and let herself noiselessly
out the back door. Rex, fortunately, was elsewhere. He would
have wanted to accompany her, and might have made a fuss.

The night had grown chill, with a restless wind. Autumn was
coming. Hilda was grateful for the coolness, but less happy
about the wind. As she made her way up the broad, tree-lined
street, the harsh arc light on the corner behind her cast shadows
of limbs, writhing and twisting on the path ahead. Somewhere
in the deep recesses of her mind Hilda's fear of trees and trolls
stirred. They were not true, of course, the old stories. She knew
that in the daylight. But in the dark . . .

She clutched her flapping cloak and hurried.

The central fire station, Patrick's base, was only a few blocks from Tippecanoe Place, but by the time she reached it, she was panting and her heart was beating fast. The firehouse was lighted by electricity, fire authorities believing it to be safer than gas (a controversial opinion). Hilda was profoundly glad to see the glow of the firehouse window.

Now that she was here, she was frightened of what she was doing. Truly it was foolish. Yes, she needed to find out all she could about the dead man, Lefkowicz, but morning would have been soon enough. She could have manufactured some excuse to leave the house, or sent a message with a delivery boy. There would have been far less risk.

However, she was here now. Stubbornness had brought her here; stubbornness would not allow her to leave without accomplishing her purpose.

Or at least making the attempt. There was always the chance that the firemen had retired for the night. Leaving a light burning? Well, they might do that, in order to see their way if an alarm should come in. Perhaps no one would answer her knock. If she could wake no one, she could go straight home, her honor satisfied.

Her luck was out, or in, depending on the point of view. It was not so very late, just after ten o'clock, and several of the firemen were sitting downstairs, playing cards. Her timid knock was answered immediately, and by Patrick himself.

"Thought you might be 'round" was his greeting.

Hilda, whose nerves were on edge, was tart. "Patrick! For why would you think such a thing, that I would come out at night to see you? You are not so important, so wonderful that I would—"

"But you did, didn't you?"

"Only because I wish information!"

"O' course. I can't ask you in, women aren't allowed in the firehouse, but we can sit on the porch for a minute." He steered her to the rocking chairs where the firemen lounged on nice days.

"Now," he said when they were settled, "you'll be wantin' to know about Lefkowicz."

"How did you know?"

"I read the papers, too, you know. I saw the name and was curious. I knew you'd be on it like a cat after a mouse."

Hilda decided to ignore the unflattering comparison. "And so?"

"So I went to the police station before I went on duty today."

"Yes, and . . . ?" She tapped her foot; her chair rocked rapidly.

"Lefkowicz wasn't there."

"*Patrick.*"

He abandoned the game. "He was his cousin," he said baldly. "The others told me. And he was the foreman on the city hall, the man who died, I mean. They said Lefkowicz—the patrolman—is in a state about it all."

"Patrick, he is a nice man. I am sorry."

"Me, too, but bein' sorry doesn't help. When I get off duty tomorrow mornin' I'm goin' to go talk to him, see if they're any closer to findin' out who did this.

"Now, don't you want to know what else I've found out?"

"Oh! You have learned more?"

"Not a lot," he admitted. "I went 'round to a couple of taverns last night and did a little talkin'. Askin' about the murders, in a casual sort of way, you know, and about Studebaker's. Nobody said anythin' about the murders to amount to a hill of beans. But the interestin' thing was, nobody knew anything about Studebaker's, either. Oh, they all said what we've said, that somethin's goin' on there, an nobody'll talk."

Hilda sat up straighter in her chair and frowned. "I do not see why that interested you. It is no different from what we already know."

"But it is, don't you see? Nobody seems to know anythin' except the men who work at Studebaker's, an' they won't talk. So whatever is happenin', it's an inside thing, see? It's not somebody from outside tryin' to start trouble, or there'd be talk of it outside."

"Hmmm." Hilda thought about that for a moment, and then

tipped herself out of her chair. "I must go, Patrick. If I am missed, I will lose my job."

"And I'm goin' to bed. I hope there's no more fires tonight. I've fought one already, and I'm tired."

"Patrick! Where? When? I did not hear fire bells—"

"About an hour ago, just down the street, some straw in a stable. It could've been bad, but we got it out in no time at all."

"Oh. Then it was not—I thought it might have been at the city hall."

"What's to burn there? It was next door." He yawned. "I'll be gettin' off at six in the mornin', me girl, an' I'll go to the police station straightaway an' talk to Lelkowicz. An' I'll find a way to get you the information, just as soon as I can."

"Oh, yes, Patrick, please!"

"Now, you'll be careful goin' back? I'd come with you, but I'm not supposed to leave here. If an alarm came in . . ."

"I will be careful. Do not worry, Patrick. Good night."

She melted into the darkness, her black cloak billowing in the wind.

11

... the cornerstone of the new city hall [was] placed into position today shortly before noon by Mayor Schuyler Colfax.
—South Bend *Tribune*, May 20, 1901

HILDA saw a small movement at the corner of the firehouse as she left, and put a hand to her mouth before she told herself not to be foolish. It was probably a cat, or a rat, or her imagination, and she must not let her imagination run free, not with the walk home still to accomplish.

So steadfastly did she refuse to dwell on the night or the terrors it might hold that she never noticed the shadow moving along the other side of Washington Street. If she had looked in that direction, she might have observed that it was too big, and the wrong shape, to be the shadow of a tree or limb, and that it was moving, not fitfully with the wind, but purposefully, staying always a few paces behind her. But she did not look.

When she reached the corner where Tippecanoe Place loomed and turned left to walk the half block to the back drive, the shadow glided silently across Washington Street. It crouched by the low fieldstone wall of the huge property until Hilda's footsteps crunched on gravel; then it moved swiftly up the lawn toward the carriage entrance of the mansion.

Hilda ran down the basement stairs and put her hand to the knob of the back door, and nearly screamed when it swung open at her touch.

"And about time, too," said Norah in a furious whisper. "I've been waitin' for you this half hour. Come away in and upstairs before we both get caught!" She closed the door, only just refraining from banging it shut, and put up the chain with a rattle.

Outside, the owner of the shadow approached the basement stairs, only to stop short as a small shape approached. Rex made no remark, but simply stood looking at the human, his nose and jowels quivering.

"At least I know now where she lives," a voice muttered at last. "I will soon know who she is. Good dog—stay."

The shadow blended with the other shadows of the night and was gone.

Patrick was as good as his word. As Hilda was helping Mrs. Sullivan with the family breakfast the next morning and trying to stifle her yawns, Anton stole into the kitchen and slipped a folded piece of paper into her hand.

"From Mr. Cavanaugh," he whispered. "He gave it to me when I took out the rubbish."

"You, Anton!" The cook turned around and fixed him with a wrathful eye. "What do you think you're doin' in me kitchen, then? There's shoes to be cleaned; be off with you!"

Hilda dropped the paper into her pocket, but the moment she was released from her kitchen duties, she stepped into the lavatory, only a few steps away, and eagerly pulled out the note.

There were only a few words. "He knows some things," Hilda read. "Meet me back door 2:00 if you can."

She tore the note into very small pieces, dropped them into the water closet, and waited until they were very soggy and settling to the bottom before she pulled the chain.

"Hmph! Took you long enough, I must say," said Mrs. Sullivan, who was waiting outside the door. "No consideration for others, you youngsters."

Colonel George Studebaker had many business interests, but as secretary of Studebaker Brothers Manufacturing he naturally spent a good deal of time at the factory. Especially with his father away, his duties kept him very busy. This morning, however, he had stayed home for a meeting with some of South Bend's leading businessmen.

It was a golden opportunity for Hilda. She had been told to wait and clean the library later, but she had no scruples whatever about keeping very quiet while she was moving about the drawing room, next door. As soon as the chance presented itself, she slipped a bronze letter opener between the heavy sliding doors that divided the two rooms and created a gap, minute, but wide enough to let sound pass through.

". . . a terrible disaster, of course." It was Colonel George's voice. Was he talking about the president? But he was doing much better, according to the butcher's boy.

"Warren may not have been exactly—well—my favorite person, but he was a sound man at his job. No telling, now, what will happen to the city hall," went on Colonel George.

Oh! The murders! Hilda pressed her ear even closer.

"What do you suppose Avery will have to say about it?" One of the other men; Hilda didn't know his voice.

"Hah!" said a third man. "If I know Avery, he won't have a good word to say for the poor fellow even at his funeral."

There was a ripple of cold laughter, with no amusement in it, and a waft of cigar smoke caught Hilda in the nose. She pressed her hand to her mouth to stifle a cough.

"Well, gentlemen," said Colonel George, "I've asked you to come here this morning, rather than to the factory, because I have a very serious and confidential matter to discuss with you. I must ask that what I am about to tell you not go beyond the walls of this room. It is not too much to say that the future of the Studebaker Brothers Manufacturing Company, nay, the very future of South Bend, may—are those doors shut?"

Hilda was out of the drawing room and around the corner into the reception room before anyone could get to the doors to make sure.

She was shaken. Here from the very horse's mouth was word that something of grave import was going on at Studebaker's. Why was the colonel talking about it? Was he about to warn other businessmen that the troubles might affect them? "The very future of South Bend . . ."

Oh, she must talk to Patrick about this! Two o'clock couldn't come soon enough!

And then the force of what she was thinking struck her like a fist, and she had to steady herself against a piece of statuary.

She couldn't talk to Patrick about what Colonel George had said. She couldn't talk to anyone at all. She might carp about her employers from time to time, but at bottom she was intensely loyal. The colonel had said that this was confidential. She could not betray that confidentiality.

Oh, how she wished that she had never heard him! She knew that listening at doors was technically wrong, but she had always viewed it as one of the privileges of servitude in a grand house. Now she began to realize why it was sometimes wiser to mind one's own business.

Her hand hurt. She looked down and saw that she was leaning heavily on the marble foot of a young George in the lovely statue of his three children that Mr. Clem had commissioned long ago. She pushed herself upright and went back to work, running her duster along the base of the statue and into the crevices and thinking furiously.

Colonel and Mrs. George both lunched away from home that day, so the servants were finished with luncheon chores early. Hilda went upstairs for her rest, sure that she wouldn't sleep a wink, and instead fell into the deep slumber of emotional exhaustion and dreamed again of men rioting, a factory in flames, the American flag falling from the topmost roof with a resounding crash . . .

She woke with a start, to hear branches outside creaking in the wind. Then that was what . . . oh! She sat straight up, looked at the clock, and swung her feet out of bed in an instant.

Five past two! Patrick! She thrust her feet into her boots and ran downstairs.

She bypassed the basement, where Mr. Williams was likely

to be snoozing in his own particular chair in the servants' room, Rex at his feet. Either might wake if she came near, and she dared not get caught. Instead she slipped out the back door of the first floor, onto the big back porch, and down the few steps to the back drive.

He was there, pacing with his back to her, out by the carriage house. She started to run to him and then thought better of it, forcing her pace to a sedate walk. She feared that her cheeks were flushed, but the wind was brisk enough to account for that.

He turned and saw her then. "I thought maybe you couldn't come out."

"I was asleep."

"Hah! An' makin' out last night like this was life or death to you!"

"If not to me, it might be to someone," she replied tartly. "Patrick. Tell me what you know, but quickly. Mr. Williams will miss me soon."

He was too full of the importance of it to tease Hilda for long. "Well," he said, gesturing for her to sit on the stone bench, "I talked to Lefkowicz. He came in to the police station early today, only to ask 'em for the day off, for the funeral. But I was just off duty, an' I'd gone down there, like I said I would, so I saw him an' talked to him for a little."

"Is he very unhappy?"

"What you'd expect. The man was family. O' course he's upset."

"Perhaps you should not have talked to him, Patrick. I did not think—I have been very foolish." Her eyes dropped to her lap.

"You are, sometimes, you know." He said it, not patronizingly, but in a matter-of-fact sort of way. "But it was all right this time, me girl, truly. He wanted to talk about it, and he said somethin' important. There was a special reason for him to be upset about the killin's. See, he feels guilty about it all."

Hilda looked up at him, eyes wide with concentration.

"He said his cousin—his Christian name was Casimir—he

said Casimir was foreman on the city hall buildin' project, an' proud of what he was doin'. But lately, he said—our Lefkowicz said, I mean—his name is Stefan—anyway, Stefan said that Casimir told him that things weren't goin' right with the work."

"Not right? What did he mean?"

"It was little things at first, he said. Materials an' tools goin' missin', maybe a bucket o' mortar here or a hod there. Mr. Warren, he thought it was some o' the men pilferin', an' he gave it to 'em, good an' hard. But it got worse. An' the worst thing was, one mornin' they all comes to work an' a whole section o' wall they'd put up the day before is wrecked, knocked down an' the stones broke, even."

"Patrick!"

"Yeah. So he—Mr. Warren—says he wants a watchman there at night, so they can catch whoever's doin' this. 'Cause it's costin' him time an' money, an' he figgers Mr. Oliver is goin' to get wind of it an' they'll all be for it. So he hires a watchman, but nothin' happens the nights he's there.

"So he pulls 'im off, an' the very first night, a load of marble gets took."

"Oh, but, Patrick, that is serious! Marble, it is very expensive."

"Yeah, and this was fine, rare stuff, not just black, but a dark green, some of it. The Olivers go for the best, you know. It was for the front entryway, Stefan said, an' it hadn't ought to've been delivered yet, but it was there, an' too heavy to shift easy, so they put a tarpaulin over it an' let it sit till they were ready for it. An' then one mornin' it's gone.

"So Mr. Warren, he's terrible riled, an' he says to Casimir, he says to 'im, we'll watch, ourselves, tonight. We'll hide, he says, an' we'll catch the—er—the men that're doin' these things. So, how Stefan knows about this, see, is, Casimir, he comes to the police station, an' he says to Stefan, quietlike ('cause they don't want the whole town to know what's happenin', see), he says to 'im will he keep his eyes open tonight—that's the Saturday, you understand. An' Stefan says he's not on duty that night, but he'll be sure to check the next night. But by that time . . . ."

Hilda was appalled. "Oh, but he must feel very bad! If he had been there . . ."

"If he'd've been there, he'd likely've been killed, too, which is what I told him, straight out. But you're right, he's feelin' like a skunk, an' he said he's goin' to find out who did this if it's the last thing he ever does."

Hilda frowned. "Patrick, I do not like it that he said that. It might be true. It might be the last thing for him."

"It might at that. For any of us, you know."

"Yes, but no one knows—the killer does not know—that we, you and I, are interested. For us it will be safe, if we are careful. And—oh, Patrick! Nearly I forgot. I have news, too."

For there was one thing she could tell Patrick from the conversation she had overheard.

"I think that Mr. Warren had enemies. Colonel George did not like him very much, I heard him say, and one of the other men—"

"What other men?"

"It does not matter. There were some men here to talk to Colonel George, and I heard—by accident, you understand."

Patrick was very careful not to grin.

"*Ja*, by accident. One of the men, he said that Mr. Avery would not say good things about Mr. Warren, even at his funeral!"

"There's people like that, you know, who never have a good word to say about anybody. It might not mean anythin' much."

"Yes, but I know Mr. Avery. I do not think he is like that. He is a very nice man, and a handsome man, too. He comes here to dinner. And, Patrick, the last time he was here, he—well, he smiled at Mrs. Warren, and . . ."

Patrick considered that. "Lots of men smile at other men's wives," he said at last. "It doesn't mean anythin'."

"You did not see the way he smiled."

"You're makin' somethin' out of nothin'! An' even if it's the way you think, that's a reason for Warren not to like Avery, not the other way 'round."

Hilda tossed her head. "It is interesting, that is all. If you do not think so, I do not care. But we will talk tomorrow? It is Wednesday." Wednesday was Hilda's half day off.

"I'll be here at two on the dot, providin' I get me sleep tonight, an' don't have to put out no fires. We'll go for a walk."

"Only for a walk," said Hilda firmly. "To talk about the murders."

"O' course!"

If Patrick had other thoughts, he kept them to himself. As for Hilda, she had already decided where they would go on their walk. It was time she talked to Patrolman Lefkowicz herself.

12

Certain it is that the utterances of Emma Goldman incited the cowardly wretch Czolgosz to do the dastardly deed of last Friday.

—South Bend *Tribune*, September 10, 1901

THE newspapers that evening provided matter for discussion around the servants' supper table. The president's condition came up, but not a great deal, as the news continued to be good, and good news, as everyone knows, is no news. According to both the Republican *Tribune* and the Democratic *Times*, all signs seemed to indicate that recovery was only a matter of time. The funeral of Roger Warren was reported in full, including a eulogy by Herbert Avery that surprised Hilda. There was a small item on page three (of the *Times*, only) about the funeral of Casimir Lefkowicz. The big news in both papers, however, was the arrest, in Chicago, of Emma Goldman.

"Who's Emma Goldman?" asked Elsie as the servants were eating their supper.

Mrs. Sullivan sighed loudly. "An' have you been livin' in Timbuktu, then, that you don't know the most notorious woman in America?"

Elsie stared, and Mr. Williams cleared his throat. "Emma Goldman, my girl, is a Russian Jewess who came to this country and was received kindly, and who has no respect for the country that offered her refuge. She has, for at least the past ten years, delivered lectures the length and breadth of this country— dreadful, appalling lectures that chill the blood. She is opposed to everything a decent woman holds dear: marriage, motherhood, and the sanctity of the home. She is an anarchist, a convicted felon, and an extremely dangerous woman. She has incited riots all over this country, and it was her influence, mind you, that instigated the dastardly assassin to make his attempt upon the life of our president!"

Elsie blinked, having understood about half the butler's passionate rhetoric. "Why did they arrest her?"

Mr. Williams lifted his hands in exasperation. "I told you, she's a dangerous anarchist! What more reason need there be?"

Hilda and Norah dared not look at each other, but the same thought was in both minds. If anarchists were being arrested just because they were anarchists, whether they'd done anything or not, what was going to happen to people like Flynn—and John Bolton?

When the two maids had finished their duties that night, they adjourned once more to Hilda's room to talk matters over.

Hilda, whose conscience, according to its own somewhat eccentric rules, was stern, had decided just what she could and could not reveal to Norah.

"Norah, I must tell you something important. We are right in what we have thought. I heard from—someone—today that something big is ready to happen, and it will be very close to us, just below our noses!"

Norah stifled a giggle. "Right under our noses, do you mean?"

"Ja, that is what I say. And if you do not understand me, what I mean is that the something will be at the Studebaker factory!"

"Sven talked to you? Or to one o' your sisters?"

"No. I cannot tell you how I know, but I do know."

"So what's goin' to happen, if you know so much?"

"That I do not know. Only that it is so terrible it may change the whole history of South Bend. That is what I heard—someone—say. It is serious, Norah!"

Norah was silent, picking at a shiny black shoe button. When she looked up at Hilda, she'd lost all inclination to giggle.

"If it's true, it's serious, all right. For all of us. How many men would be out of work if Studebaker's went on strike? Your brother, two o' mine, lots o' me cousins—someone in nearly every family around here. And if it's that bad—the person you heard, is it someone who really knows?"

"Oh, yes," said Hilda fervently.

"Then if it's so bad, did you ever stop to think what might become of us if the worst happened?"

"To us—oh, Norah, you do not think Studebaker's could fail?"

Her voice held absolute horror. Such a thing was unthinkable. South Bend had many industries, but the two giants were Studebaker's and Oliver's. They had been there for years, for decades. They would always be there. The wealth they generated was beyond comprehension, and could never melt away.

"This house . . ." said Hilda, looking around her.

Even here on the top floor, in a small servant's bedroom, wealth was evident. The walls were nicely wainscoted. The floor was plain, but solid and beautifully laid. The windows fit tightly, the door was substantial, with massive hardware. Furniture, rug, curtains, all were plain in design but well made. There was a steam radiator; Tippecanoe Place was centrally heated, and Studebaker servants, unlike their counterparts in many houses, were warm in winter. Why, the butler even had a handsome fireplace in his room, and coal enough to burn in it, too.

"Surely they would not . . ." Hilda couldn't finish.

"If they lost their money, they'd have to, wouldn't they?"

It was a dreadful thought to take to bed, and Hilda slept badly despite her weariness. The weather changed in the night, growing warmer; that didn't help. Before her alarm shrilled, long before dawn broke, she was awake and worrying. This problem had too many angles to it, that was the trouble. Her attention was being drawn in too many directions.

There was the immediate threat to Studebaker's, and by implication, to the household of Tippecanoe Place and to hundreds of other households all over South Bend. Or no, it spread wider than that even. There were Studebaker dealers all over the country, indeed, all over the world. Studebaker Brothers was the largest supplier of wagons on the planet. Farmers in Europe and South America, in Africa and India, depended upon the reliable green-and-red wagons. And then there were the carriages—President McKinley, himself, had a Studebaker carriage—and the buggies and the delivery trucks and the street-sweeping wagons and the fire trucks. . . . Hilda was overwhelmed by the possible repercussions of a failure of the Studebaker Brothers Manufacturing Company. But what could she, one woman of no importance whatever, do to prevent trouble there?

Then there was the worry about Flynn Murphy and John Bolton. If she and Norah knew that the two men had expressed opinions and engaged in actions that were unwise, to say the least, then other people knew, too. And if they talked . . . Hilda shuddered. In the climate of anti-anarchist hysteria created by the assassin's bullets, both men could be arrested on the feeblest of charges. Scandal! If nothing worse, she thought darkly.

And how did all this connect with the deaths, in South Bend, of a contractor and his foreman? For there was a connection, she was convinced, else what was the grim significance of the red, white, and blue shroud?

And how was she to find out anything more about any of these things?

"I would be happier if I had more time to myself," she grumbled to Norah as they headed down the back stairs an hour later, carrying their lidded chamber pots. (There were no bathrooms on the top floor.)

"We've more than most," said Norah, surprised. "Our half days, and every Sunday off instead of every other. An' a rest in the afternoon; there's not many servants get that."

Hilda sighed. "I know. We are treated well. All the same, how can I look into problems when I must be here all of the time?"

Norah shrugged. "Count your blessin's, girl. Look at your sisters, an' mine, an' all the dailies. They leave off doin' one job an' go home to do another. We're lucky to live in."

Hilda sighed again. "Yes, I suppose you are right. It is a good job, and a comfortable home, but it is like a jail."

"Hah! I don't notice you havin' much trouble gettin' out o' the jail when you've a mind to!"

For once Hilda was silenced.

She went about her duties that morning with breathless efficiency. The work must be done perfectly, for in only two days, now, the master and mistress of the house would return. They had been away too long; Hilda had missed them. They were very particular and could be hard to please, but there was reassurance in their presence. If Mr. Clem were there, nothing could possibly happen to the company he and his brothers had founded. Not that Colonel George wasn't a pleasant man, or a capable one, but it wasn't the same. Mr. Clem *was* Studebaker's. His one surviving brother, J.M., was a good man, but it was Mr. Clem's hand at the helm that had always kept crises at bay.

Or at least that was Hilda's opinion.

As she was changing to her street clothes after lunch she made plans, and as soon as she was ready, she tapped on Norah's door.

"It is me, Hilda. I come in, *ja*?" And she did.

Norah was struggling into her corset. Like Hilda, she never wore it while she was working, and seldom when she went out, either. Hilda viewed her with dismay.

"You do not go home to your family this afternoon?"

"Not today. The weather's turned fine again. We'll not have much more o' summer, and I'm not spendin' it indoors. I'm walkin' out with Sean."

Sean O'Neill was Norah's on-again, off-again beau. Apparently, he was now on again.

"Oh," said Hilda. "I had hoped you would see your family."

"An' why?"

"Norah, I think hard this morning. All morning, while I work, I think about all the problems."

"It's a wonder you don't have one o' your headaches, then. There's nothing very sweet to think about, if you ask me."

"You are right. And in the end what I think is that I cannot solve all these problems by myself."

"And that's a wonder, it is! You've always thought you could, before!" The discomfort of her corset always gave Norah a sharp tongue.

"Yes, but I have been wrong. And there is too much, too many directions, too—" Her hands flew in agitated circles as her English fell short.

"It's all too complicated, is what I suppose you're meanin'."

"Yes. Thank you! And that is why I need you to help me, and Patrick, and my sisters, and everyone I can—can persuade, is that the word?"

"It's the word, all right. And what is it you're goin' to try to persuade me to do?"

"Norah, you must make your brothers talk. We must know what is planned, what is to happen."

"Hah! You don't know Flynn. When he shuts up, he shuts up tight."

"I did not mean Flynn. I do not speak now of the trouble he is in. I mean the Studebaker trouble. Two of your brothers work there. You must learn what the trouble is!"

"You have a brother there, too. Can you make him talk?"

"No, but he is Swedish. Swedes do not talk like the Irish."

Norah laughed, though in somewhat stifled fashion. "That's true enough, though you can talk enough for two. All right, I'll do me best, but they'll all be workin' this afternoon. It'll have to wait till Sunday, supposin' I can get anybody to say a word."

"You will make them talk, Norah, and as soon as you can. I look to you and Patrick to answer the Studebaker question. Me, I go to solve a murder!" She tripped down the back stairs to meet Patrick.

"And where shall we go, then? To the park?"

He offered his arm. Hilda ignored it, as she usually did. "To the police station, please, Patrick."

"Ah, Hilda! Look at that blue sky! I thought we'd go to the park, maybe take a boat on the river." She did not respond. He sighed. "They'll not like you pokin' your oar in."

Hilda frowned. "What is this, please?"

"Sorry. 'Pokin' your oar in' means meddlin' with somethin' that's none of your affair." He saw her face change, and added hastily, "I don't say I'm sayin' that, but it's what they'll say. The police don't like outsiders buttin' in, and they're none too fond of you, anyway, on account of you showed 'em up the last time."

"That is why you come with me." She started down the drive. "They will be polite to you."

Patrick wasn't too sure of that, but when Hilda made up her mind, trying to get her to change it was a waste of breath. He looked up, lifted his hands as if in apology to the lovely day that was going to be wasted, and fell into step beside Hilda.

She laid out her campaign as they walked. "Patrick, we must know t'ree t'ings." She shook her head with irritation and repeated, carefully, "Three things. We must know what Leon Czolgosz said and did when he was here. We must know what is planned for Studebaker's, and for the other big factories. And we must know who killed Mr. Warren and Mr. Lefkowicz, and why."

"Is *that* all?"

"Yes," she said in surprise. "Do you think of other things?"

"Ah, forget it! You'll remember, won't you, that the police are already tryin' to find out most o' those things?"

Hilda nodded. "But you know about the police in South Bend, Patrick."

He did. Everyone knew that many policemen could be bought—small wonder, really, considering what they were paid. And there were a few who, even without a bribe, would turn a blind eye, at best, and actively cooperate, at worst, when violence to immigrants was threatened. South Bend was a city of many foreigners, a true melting pot, but not everyone thought that the immigrants were assets to the community.

"I cannot learn all these things by myself, Patrick. I will ask others for help, and what I can do myself, I will do. Now. I have asked Norah to learn what she can about Studebaker's, and I wish you, Patrick, to do the same—in taverns and other places where men gather, as we have said."

"I've already tried. I got nowhere."

"There are other taverns, Patrick. Also, I wish you to talk to your friends about the city hall and the troubles about the building."

"I can do that, but what are you plannin' for yourself?"

"Me, I go with you to the police station to talk to Patrolman Lefkowicz, and after that I talk to John Bolton."

13

... the people are paying sums to be protected in life and property, but are not getting all they pay for .... With such conditions a woman is not safe on the streets of South Bend unless she is accompanied by an escort and possibly not then.

—South Bend *Tribune*, April 5, 1898

HILDA would never have admitted to Patrick just how glad she was that he was by her side when they entered the police station. She hated the place, with its stale smells of tobacco and sweat, its spittoons and the stains that surrounded them, its vaguely threatening atmosphere. If she had been alone, she knew she might have been treated with discourtesy, or worse. With Patrick it was all very much easier.

He left her on a relatively clean chair in the hall and sauntered up to the front desk.

"Lefkowicz here today? Or did he take the day off?"

"He's here." The officer at the desk jerked his head toward the back of the building, and Patrick, with a *stay there* gesture to Hilda, walked away and presently returned, Patrolman Lefkowicz following him.

"How do you do, Miss Johansson?" he said formally.

"Miss Johansson is wantin' to ask you some questions," said Patrick quietly. "I'm thinkin' it'd be better to go outside?"

"Yes. This is not a good place for a lady." The policeman led the way to a bench in the sunshine. They all sat down, and he looked inquiringly at Hilda.

Hilda in turn looked at him, and thought he looked wretched. His face was white and strained; his hands picked nervously at the buttons on his uniform.

"You have not slept." It was not what she had meant to say.

"No. Not well. How may I help you, Miss Johansson?"

She had planned a subtle approach, but this man was suffering. He deserved as brief a series of questions as she could frame.

"I wish some information about—I am sorry to cause you pain—about the deaths of Mr. Warren and your cousin. I believe the police do little about these crimes, and I worry."

Lefkowicz sighed. "We are all doing what we can, but there is little evidence. And, of course, they care mostly about Mr. Warren."

"Yes!" Hilda kept her voice low, but she spoke with intensity. "They do not care about the death of an immigrant. Especially—I am sorry to say it, but you know it is true—especially a Pole."

He nodded wearily. "The assassin—I cannot bring myself to speak his name—he is a Pole, and that is not good for any of us."

"Yes! You understand! I think we must help one another, we who have come here to this country, must protect each other when times are bad. This is a bad time, Mr. Lefkowicz."

Again he nodded.

"So I wish you to tell me anything you know about the death of your cousin and his employer. For unless we can learn who did this terrible thing, there will be—there could be—the people of South Bend might . . ."

"They might rise up against us," he said, very softly. "It is best to say things plainly."

"You are right." She nodded emphatically.

"Miss Johansson, I would like to help you. I know you have skill in finding things out."

"You weren't on duty on Sunday, were you?" said Patrick, who had allowed Hilda her head until now.

"No, or I would have known at once that it was my cousin who had died. But I never even saw him until he was—was laid out." His voice shook for only a moment before he had himself once more under rigid control. "It was one of the other laborers who identified him. Myself, I know nothing I have not said to my friends in the police over and over again." He took a deep breath. "My cousin went to the city hall building site that night, with Mr. Warren, to try to find out who was sabotaging the construction. The next day they were found dead."

"Your cousin, did he have an idea who the thief might be?" asked Hilda.

"If he did, he said nothing to me. We were good friends, Casimir and I, almost like brothers, but he was older and he did not often talk to me about important things. I think, though, from little things Casimir said, that Mr. Warren himself knew who the person was, or had a good idea."

"But if he knew, why did he place himself and your cousin in such danger that night?"

"I think because he could prove nothing. He told Casimir that no one would ever believe him. If they caught the man in the act, you see, they would be able to take him to the police."

"It was a very foolish thing to do!"

Patrick nodded grim agreement.

"Yes, but how were they to know the man—or men, it might have been—would kill? It makes no sense, Miss Johansson, and I have thought about it and thought about it until my brain has stopped working at all. These thefts, they were a nuisance, but little more than that. The person responsible would have been fined and made to replace the stolen materials. He might even have been sentenced to a little time in jail, but . . . to kill over something so petty . . ." His voice broke, and he covered his face with his hands.

"I am sorry," said Hilda gently. "I did not mean to upset you, but you have told me one important thing. I think I must talk to Mr. Warren's family."

"There is no family, only his wife, and I do not think she will talk to you."

"Oh. Yes, I suppose . . . she grieves, now, and it is not a good time . . ."

"Myself, I am not so sure she is grieving. She is acting—odd."

All Hilda's senses came to the alert. "How, odd?"

"I am not sure; I cannot put it in words. I was one of those who went to tell her about her husband's death, and she wept and cried, as one would expect, but she also seemed very nervous. Her hands . . ." The patrolman's own hands fluttered in imitation. "I am sorry I cannot tell you more. It was only an impression."

"I think it was very smart of you to notice anything, in your own grief!" said Hilda warmly.

"I did not yet know about my cousin."

"Oh." She could find nothing to say in the face of Lefkowicz's quiet dignity. Decency demanded that she leave him alone to deal with his loss. But there was so much more that she needed to know.

"Mr. Lefkowicz, what do the police think? Do they have ideas, do they follow trails?"

"I do not think they have any ideas, really. They—we—have asked all the neighbors if they saw or heard anything, but there was the storm—thunder, lightning. They were only trying to sleep through all that noise. They heard nothing else, and saw nothing at all."

"Is that all they have done? Ask the neighbors?"

Lefkowicz looked at the ground. "I would not like you to think that the police have always been this way. Before this superintendent came . . . but no, that is not all they have done. Also they have asked at the train stations, to see if any suspicious strangers have come to town in the past few days. And they are checking to see if there are any known anarchists in town—because of the flag, you see."

Hilda's heart pounded; she dared not look at Patrick. "Yes, the flag," she said quickly. "That is my last question. What do you know about the flag? Why would someone do such a wicked thing?"

"We have asked ourselves that, many times. We do not know."

Hilda took a deep breath. "Mr. Lefkowicz, where is that flag?"

"At the station, unless it has been returned to its owner."

"You know who owns it?" Hilda's voice was sharp with excitement.

Lefkowicz sighed a little and shook his head. "Yes, we know, and it is of no help. It belongs to the man who lives next door to the new city hall. He took it down—"

"Next door?" said Patrick, interrupting. "The livery stables?"

"Yes, the owner lives above them, you know."

"I know," said Patrick. "He's had a run of bad luck lately. There was a little fire there Monday night. We put it out fast enough, but—"

"Patrick! Always you like to talk of fires! I wish to learn about the flag!"

Patiently, Lefkowicz continued where he had left off. "The man took it down the night of the murder, when we had that little bit of rain—do you remember? He was afraid it would rain hard later, as it did, and he did not want the flag getting soaked. He did not think it respectful. So he took it down from the pole and folded it, and left it on his front porch, and when he went to put it up on Sunday morning it was gone. He reported the theft to us, and it was obvious what had happened."

"But it is not so obvious *why* it happened!" Hilda chewed her lip for a moment. "Mr. Lefkowicz, what happened to the flag? Where is it now?"

"We spread it out to dry. It was wet when they found it, of course. We'll need to get it back to the owner, but it should be washed and ironed first."

That was her opportunity. "I can do that for you. I am not a laundress, but I know how to do laundry. I have done enough, at home in Sweden."

The patrolman looked dubious. "I am not sure I ought to let it leave the station."

"What harm can it do? And it will save your men some work, men, I think, who do not know how to wash such a thing. Please, Mr. Lefkowicz!"

He was not the first man to succumb to the force of a pair of melting blue eyes. Patrick was not at all surprised when, five minutes later, Hilda had the flag, tucked into a feed sack, under her arm.

They made their thanks to Patrolman Lefkowicz and left the station.

"And what're you goin' to do with that?"

"I go home to study it! You, Patrick, you go to ask questions. We will talk tomorrow!"

14

You know my methods, Watson.
　　—Sir Arthur Conan Doyle, "The Crooked Man"

THE great mansion was sleeping like a cat in the sunshine when Hilda crept in at the back door, listened anxiously for a moment, and then tiptoed up the steep stairs to her room on the top floor. There was no particular reason for her to tiptoe. She had a perfect right to return early from her afternoon out if she wished to do so, and if she was carrying a parcel, that was no one else's business. But if Mr. Williams were to see her, ask her what she had under her arm . . . no, stealth was wiser.

Once she was safely in her room with the door locked, she breathed more freely. It was very hot in the small room with the western sun pouring in, but it was private. She wasted no time fretting about the heat, but carefully unwrapped her bundle.

The flag was dirty and wrinkled and stained. It smelled musty and sweet at the same time, and there was another, faintly metallic odor. Hilda's insides reacted unhappily to the knowledge of what the stains and the odors represented, but she sternly told her stomach to behave, spread the flag out on the floor, and knelt to examine it.

The flag was a large one, probably six feet long, and made of a good wool bunting. It was nearly new. Hilda studied with a critical housemaid's eye the sturdy cloth, the firm, even stitching, still clean except for where mud and blood had been ground in.

It had been treated shamefully. There were mud stains running in an irregular line a foot or so from both long edges. Another brown stain darkened part of the blue field and several of the forty-five white stars.

Hilda turned her eyes deliberately away from that dark blotch, frowned, and looked more closely at the mud stains. There was something odd about their pattern. She would have expected mud all over the part of the flag that had lain under the murdered man, in contact with the ground, but there was no large patch of mud anywhere, only the jagged lines of staining near the edges. Drat! She ought to have asked Patrolman Lefkowicz how the flag had been draped when it was found.

She sat back on her heels and pursed her lips. The flag was less wrinkled in the center than on the edges. There was something familiar about the middle of that flag. . . .

Yes! That time she'd been caught in the rain, and hadn't been able to get home before her clothes had dried on her. That slightly rough appearance, with a crease here and there where her body caused folds, looked just as the center of the flag looked.

Well, that made sense. It had rained hard the night the men were murdered. The flag would have been soaked, and then would have dried gradually, the part that was on top, at least.

But that meant the edges must have been the part under Mr. Warren's body. That made sense, too. If the man had been struck down first, the murderer wouldn't have lifted him up, carefully spread the flag on the ground like a sheet, and put the body on top. No. He would have laid the flag over the body like a blanket and tucked the edges under so it wouldn't be blown away.

It was a horrid picture. Hilda licked her dry lips, once again admonished her stomach, and deliberated some more. Her scenario seemed correct up to a point, but there was a flaw in it. If the edges of the soaking-wet flag had lain under the body all night, there ought to be hard, deep creases, and there were not. The wrinkles were more the sort that one found on the back of a skirt in damp weather: small, soft wrinkles, but easily ironed out.

That meant . . . Hilda groped for it . . . that meant the flag had not been wet when it was wrapped around poor Mr. Warren! That would explain the mud stains, too. If the rain had come after the murders, Mr. Warren's body had lain, not on mud, but on dry ground, the rain seeping only around the edges and creating those muddy lines, like ridges.

Had she discovered the time of the murder?

It was, she was certain, before the rain. When had the rain come that night?

She had lain awake that Saturday night, the pain in her head driving away the sleep she needed so badly. There had been— yes! There had been the little shower, the one that had lasted only a few minutes and had not, she remembered with growing excitement, even really wet the dust near the carriage house. It would have barely dampened a flag. That had been . . . when? About ten-thirty?

That, Mr. Lefkowicz had said, was when the man who owned the flag had taken it down and put it on the front porch. And then the real rain, cool and blessedly refreshing, had come about an hour later.

So the murders had occurred between ten-thirty and eleven-thirty! She gathered up the flag, refolded it carefully, put it back into the feed sack, and pushed it to the very back of her wardrobe. She would not wash it just yet. It could be important proof!

Proof of what?

She took off her skirt and waist, hung them carefully in the wardrobe, and lay on the bed in her shift to think that out. She considered that she had been very clever to work out the time span, but now what would happen?

She could tell the police. They might believe her or they might not. Patrolman Lefkowicz would, but he had no authority.

And if they did believe her, what then? Would they begin to narrow their focus, look harder for anarchists, torture them when they found them? The newspapers had said that Leon Czolgosz had been questioned in a "sweatbox." Hilda had only the vaguest idea what that was, but she shuddered at just the idea.

Would they uncover John's activities, and Flynn's?

She twisted on her bed, aghast at the possibilities. What if John were questioned about the night of the murder? She knew where he had been for at least part of the fateful evening. He and Flynn and a handful of others had been here, here in the Tippecanoe Place carriage house, holding a frightened meeting to try to cover up their acquaintance with an assassin. Would they tell? Would they betray each other? Or would they refuse to say, in order to protect the others, knowing that a refusal would raise suspicions?

When had that meeting begun, and how long had it lasted? If it had gone on until after the rain started, the real rain, they were all safe. But if it had ended earlier . . .

She got up and reached for her skirt. She needed facts, and she could get them from John.

Footsteps running, stumbling up the stairs. Strangled sobs. The creak and slam of a door, the jangle of bedsprings.

Half dressed, Hilda darted from her room and pulled open Norah's door.

"Norah! What is the matter?"

Norah raised her tearstained face from her pillow. "It's Flynn! They've taken Flynn!"

The story came out in bits and pieces, between sobs. Norah could supply few details.

"I don't know! All I know is, he started a fight at the mill, and it got so bad they called the police, and they put him in jail!"

Hilda threw herself down in the hard chair by Norah's bed. "But, Norah! He has been in jail for fighting before, and he will be again, probably. For what do you upset yourself?"

Norah wailed. "They put him in jail for fightin', but once they got him there, they accused him of the murders!"

She collapsed on the bed again; sobs shook the springs. Hilda stood up and went to the door.

"You're not leavin' me!"

"I am sorry, but I must hurry."

"To do what?"

"Oh," said Hilda, surprised. "I go to get Flynn out of jail, of course."

There was now no more than an hour or two of her afternoon left to her, and she must, in that time, try to do the impossible.

Hilda burst into the police station with none of her earlier timidity; the screen door hit the wall with a bang. "Where is Patrolman Lefkowicz?" she demanded.

The surly desk clerk frowned. "He's busy. We got us a murderer! You'd best just go about your business—"

"How does one find the jail cells?"

"Lefkowicz isn't back there, he's—miss, you can't go back there—look here!—"

Hilda knew that the jail cells were at the back of the building. She swept past him with fierce determination.

There was a good deal of confusion in the police station or she would have been stopped much sooner. Men, some in uniform, some in ordinary dress, hurried past, not even seeing her. In one room several men were gathered, talking. One wore a top hat; she thought she recognized the publisher of the *Tribune*.

She would probably have reached the cells if she had not literally run into Patrolman Lefkowicz first. She collided with him as he rushed out of a doorway.

"Oh, miss, I am sorry—Miss Johansson! You must not be here, we cannot allow—"

"Mr. Lefkowicz! You must tell me at once. Why have you accused Mr. Murphy of murder?"

The patrolman looked acutely unhappy. "Hush! Come with me!"

With scant ceremony, he grasped Hilda's arm and pulled her through the back door of the station and out into the alley, among the ash barrels. "I cannot talk now," he said in an undertone. "I must go back, and you must leave."

"I will not leave until you tell me why you have accused Mr. Murphy!"

"*Lower your voice!*" It was an urgent stage wisper. "I myself have accused him of nothing except disorderly behavior. I was called to the scene at the mill. He was fighting and shouting and making wild statements about strikes and anarchy and I do not remember what, so we had to arrest him. He nearly started a riot. And he has said such terrible things since, here in the jail, that the superintendent thinks he must have killed the men. And—oh, I should not tell you this, but I do not think he is the murderer! Now go! Quickly, before . . ."

He did not finish the sentence, but darted back inside, closing the door behind him. Hilda followed, or tried to follow. The door was locked.

She had not expected to accomplish her goal easily, but she had expected to get a little more information. She sighed. It was quite obvious that there was nothing more to be gained at the police station, not now, at any rate. No one would listen to her. At least Mr. Lefkowicz believed in Flynn's innocence and might be able to plant some doubt in more influential minds. As for her, she now had only one recourse.

She extricated herself from the dirty alley with as little damage to her skirts as possible and made her way back to Tippecanoe Place and straight to the carriage house. John might be out, exercising the horses . . . but he was not. He was in the tack room polishing harness, and looked up with surprise as she hurried into the room.

She didn't let him so much as speak. "John! I must know, and quickly! When did the meeting end?"

He stopped, rag in one hand, bit in the other, and looked blank. "What meeting?"

"THE meeting. The night of the murders. You and Flynn and the others."

"Oh. Don't know. Don't remember. Why?"

"*Think!* It rained that night, once for only a little time and then harder, for most of the night. Did the meeting begin before the first rain, or after?"

"Oh, before. I do remember that little sprinkle, now that you mention it. Not enough to do any good. And then—yes, we broke up just before the real rain set in. I remember now. It was thundering, and the men wanted to get home before the storm broke. Why?"

Hilda sank down on an old straight chair, her hopes dashed. "It does not matter."

"It mattered like 'Hail, Columbia' a minute ago. What's the matter?" He put his work down and fixed her with his eye. "Come on, Hilda. Talk."

Was there any reason not to tell him? She wasn't sure she could trust him, but perhaps it was better for him to know. It did concern him, after all.

"They have arrested Flynn," she said dully. "He caused a fight at the mill, but now they think he killed the two men. He is in jail for murder."

There was a moment of shocked silence, but John was quick to grasp the implications.

"You hoped the meeting had lasted longer? Why?"

"The murders happened before the rain, the hard rain."

"How do you know that?" He snapped his fingers. "Of course! The men—Lefkowicz and Warren—would've gone home as soon as it started to pour. Plain as the nose on your face!"

Hilda could have wept. All her careful reasoning over the flag to prove the obvious. She sighed wearily. "Yes. So if the meeting had ended after the rain started . . . but it did not."

"Yes, but wait a minute!" John sounded excited. "It wasn't long before the rain that we broke up! Let me think." He hitched one leg up on the workbench and mumbled to himself for a time that seemed to Hilda's tightened nerves to last for hours.

"Here, listen," he said at last. "I've been thinking it out. Flynn stayed behind for a bit after the others left. He lives the closest, you see, and—well, he'd brought the beer and he wanted to finish a bottle, so I had one with him. And after he left, I cleared away the bottles—not wanting Colonel George to see them, you understand."

Hilda looked severe, and John had the grace to look ashamed of himself.

"And then I went straight to bed, being a bit—well—"

"Drunk."

"Well . . . anyway, by the time I was climbing into bed, it was raining, hard. It sent me right off to sleep."

"That, and the drink," said Hilda. But she was not as harsh as she might have been. "Then, John, Flynn would not have had time . . ."

"I don't see how. The question is, will the police agree with us?"

15

Never allow [your servants] to enter into conversation with
each other in your presence.
—Richard A. Wells, *Manners Culture and Dress*, 1891

HILDA looked at John with new respect. "You would go to
the police and tell them? It could be dangerous for you."
John scowled. "I can't let Flynn hang for something he
didn't do, can I?"

"No, but listen to me, John. You cannot go and tell them
about the meeting."

"Watch me!"

"*No!* You do not t'ink—think. They will not let Flynn go. They
think they have their man, and they will not like to have to work
harder again. The superintendent, he is a lazy man, I think, and a
stupid one. And if you tell them about the meeting, he will
yoost—just—put all of you in jail, too. No, but I have a plan."

"Oh, do you? Well, then, we've nothing to worry about, have
we?"

Hilda ignored the sarcasm. "Yes, we must still worry, but if
my plan is good, we will worry less. We must persuade Colonel
George to get Flynn out of jail."

"Oh, of course! We just waltz up to him and—"

"No. Do not be stupid. This is the way we will do it."

She had to argue her plan with true Swedish stubbornness,
but John was at last persuaded, if reluctantly. They left the carriage house like conspirators, peering out the door to left and
right before venturing out.

"Wait!" John put out a sturdy arm to bar the doorway. "What was that?"

Hilda ducked under the arm and looked where he pointed. "I see nodding. Nothing," she corrected herself.

John relaxed. "I thought I saw someone in the lilacs, just there, by the corner of the carriage house. But there's nothing. My mind's playing tricks. Let's go, if we must."

Norah's aid had to be enlisted as well. Hilda trudged up to the top of the house to find that her friend had cried herself to sleep. Hilda hated to wake her, but she was essential to success. When Hilda had explained what Norah was to do, and was sure she could carry it off, the two of them crept downstairs to the servants' room, where John joined them.

"This is the best time," Hilda whispered. "They are just finishing their supper, and Mr. Williams and Mrs. Sullivan are upstairs. Are you ready?"

John nodded. Norah giggled nervously. Hilda shushed her, and they moved out of the room into the narrow hallway just outside the butler's pantry—and the open door to the family dining room, where Colonel and Mrs. George were peacefully finishing their casual, servantless Wednesday supper.

Hilda listened for a moment. ". . . have thought Avery was Warren's best friend. I despise hypocrisy." It was Colonel George's bass rumble.

"Yes, dear, but people are hypocritical at funerals. Speak no ill of the dead, you know."

Silence fell. Hilda administered a sharp jab in the ribs to Norah, who uttered a melodramatic wail and a loud sob. "Oh, Hilda, I don't know what I'm goin' to do. With Flynn in jail and all, I'm that upset, I can't hardly do me work! But I don't see as I can give notice. Me family needs the money too bad, now that Flynn . . ." Reality invaded melodrama. Norah's sobs became more genuine.

Hilda put an arm around her in real compassion, but her voice, too, was pitched extra loud. "Oh, Norah, do not worry. We will find a way to have Flynn released from jail. We all know that he would never do a thing so bad as murder."

"But the police'll never believe the likes of us," Norah cried in something very like true terror. "We're not important enough."

That was John's cue. "They'll have to believe us," he thundered. "I can prove Flynn was nowhere near the city hall when those men were killed. He was with me!"

"But why should the police believe *you?* You're not but a coachman," said Norah, her voice rising higher and higher.

Colonel George appeared in the doorway. Hilda restrained a sigh of relief.

"Hilda, Norah, what's all this hullabaloo?"

"Oh, sir! I am sorry, sir, we did not mean to disturb you. We did not know that you were still eating. It is yoost that Norah—but we must not trouble you. We will go away."

Norah was crying in earnest now. She pulled a handkerchief from her pocket and hid her face while she sobbed.

Mrs. George had joined her husband. She had far more experience than he in dealing with the servants. "Norah," she said crisply, "stop crying and tell me what the trouble is."

"Please, madam," said Hilda, who was determined to keep the situation under her control, "Norah's brother Flynn has been arrested for the murder of Mr. Warren and Mr. Lefkowicz. We know he did not do such a bad t'ing, but we are only servants. They will not listen to us. Norah worries very much, and she is afraid she will have to give up her yob . . ."

"Nonsense!" Mrs. George knew a domestic crisis when she saw one. Well-trained servants were hard to find, and with her in-laws coming home in two days, Norah had to be calmed down in a hurry. "Norah, is this true?"

Norah nodded mutely.

"And you, John. You say the Murphy boy was with you?"

"Yes, madam. All the evening."

"Well, then, it seems clear enough. George, you'll have a word with the police, will you?"

Colonel George raised his eyebrows and his hands in the classic "anything for a quiet life" gesture and strode back into the dining room.

"Oh, t'ank you, madam! It is good of you to take an interest, madam."

"Yes, well, look after her, will you, Hilda? Norah, do stop crying! You'll give yourself a headache."

Mrs. George also retreated, closing the door behind her. Hilda uttered that heartfelt sigh at last and hustled the other two away.

"Couldn't we just have asked them to help?" said Norah when her sobs had subsided to sniffles. "I don't see why we had to go through all that rigmarole."

"It was better this way," said Hilda firmly. "To a polite servant they can say no. With a servant who threatens to leave, they will sometimes lose their temper. But with a servant who weeps, they must find their own solution, and then they will feel clever and generous. Rich people like to feel that way.

"We must talk, but later. Now you must wash your face, Norah. If Mr. Williams learns what we have done . . ."

She didn't need to finish the thought. They all repaired to the kitchen, where Norah dashed water on her face and they foraged in the pantry and the icebox for their own supper.

The three could not talk around the supper table, with the other servants coming in and out, but as soon as supper was cleared away they drifted, by design, out of Mr. Williams's sight.

"The state dining room!" Hilda whispered, and beckoned.

The big dining room where the Studebakers held their grandest dinner parties was all the way at the other end of the house from the kitchen—perfect for a private chat.

The sun had set long since, and the only light in the cavernous room came from the gas fixtures in the reception room just outside. Hilda groped for the chairs that lined the room; the three sat down.

Hilda opened her mouth, but John spoke before she could do so. "And what are we doing here, Your Royal Highness, *if* I may make so bold as to ask? I've work to do in the stables. Besides, I was willing to help you with your playacting back there, if it was to spring Flynn, but I never said I'd be at your beck and call forever!"

Hilda frowned and tapped her foot. "You must speak more quiet, John. And do not be silly. We plan, of course."

"Plan what?" Norah and John spoke simultaneously.

"How we find the real murderer!" Hilda was growing impatient with the two of them.

"But if Colonel George gets Flynn out—"

Hilda did not allow her to finish.

"Norah, you do not think! Flynn will be free, but only for a time, only—what is the word?"

"Out on bail, I suppose you mean," growled John.

"Yes. If we do not learn who the real murderer is, Flynn will still be suspected. He will have a trial. The judge, the jury—they will be American citizens, not immigrants."

Hilda liked to talk, but she also knew when to stop talking. She let the remark lie there in the dusky room.

"Well, then, what do you want us to do?" John's voice was much more subdued.

"You, John, you must talk to Flynn, and to the others who were at the meeting—I do not remember their names—"

"Kovacz and Kapinski and Sobieski. You're not saying I should get them together again?"

"No! No, that would be a foolish thing to do. You must talk to them separately. Where do they work? Where do they live?"

"They all live near here, just off Washington Street. Kapinski works at the woolen mill with Flynn, Sobieski at Oliver's, and Kovacz—well, he was working for Warren on the city hall. I suppose he's out of work now, until they can get the building started again."

"Then it will be easy for you to talk to them. You have more freedom than Norah and me. Start with Mr. Kovacz; he will know the most, maybe."

"You want me to ask him about Warren?"

"And about the city hall, the troubles there—you know about the troubles?"

He didn't; Hilda had to tell him, briefly. "Mr. Warren did not want anyone to know, but it does not matter now. Also, ask him if he knows anything else—about any other bad things that happen."

"That all?"

"That is all now. Later, maybe, there will be other things."

"Hmmph! Dunno when I'm to get my work done."

Hilda might have said that he had little enough to do in the normal course of things, but she forbore. She wanted his cooperation. She smiled sweetly. "You do not mind a little extra work, for Flynn's sake."

He simply grunted at that.

"And, Norah, you will talk to other servants when you can. Learn all you can about Mr. Warren, and about Mr. Lelkowicz, if anyone knows him. And of course you will talk to Flynn, as soon as he is home. Try to make him tell you what is planned at Studebaker's. He might talk to you now, if he is afraid enough."

"I'll see he gets the fear o' God put in him right enough, if he *is* twice my size! Scarin' us all like that! He'll talk to me, or else!"

"And what are you going to do while we're out talking ourselves silly?" John wasn't going to let Hilda have it all her way.

"Me, I will talk to Mrs. Warren. I know her maid. And of course Patrick will learn things and tell me."

"Seems to me you're setting yourself the easiest job."

"Oh, John, do not be so—so—*difficult!* It is not important who does what thing. It is important that we learn the truth, and quick! For if we do not . . ."

Once again she let silence finish for her, and this time it was allowed to sink undisturbed into the gloom.

16

[The mistress] must be regular in her own habits . . . attentive to the details of housekeeping, economical, just, active, and considerate.
—Mrs. E. F. Ellet, ed., *The Practical Housekeeper*, 1871

FOR the rest of the evening, Hilda considered the assignment she had given herself. She could easily justify calling on Ingrid Lindahl, Mrs. Warren's maid. If they were not the best of friends, they were certainly on visiting terms. A brief visit of condolence for the death of her master would be entirely appropriate.

The problem was, when?

Today was Wednesday. Her next official free time wasn't until Sunday, and with Mr. and Mrs. Clem coming home in two days, she knew Mr. Williams would never let her take extra time off. And she couldn't wait until Sunday! She had every confidence that Colonel George would be able to see to Flynn's release, but the respite was temporary. The trial would be scheduled soon, and she had to know who the real killer was before then.

She would simply have to manufacture an errand.

Her chance came the next morning. She and Norah were rehanging the draperies in the main reception room when Mrs. George came down the magnificent staircase.

"Oh, Norah, the colonel wished you to know that your brother has been released."

Norah dropped her end of the heavy velvet panel and scrambled down the ladder, mumbling an apology, to pick it up. She curtsied awkwardly. "Thank you, madam. Please say thank you to Colonel George for me. Sure and it's very good news, madam!"

"Yes, Norah, but you know that Flynn is still in serious trouble. We must simply hope that the police will discover who the killer really is before the trial."

Norah licked her lips. "And when is that to be, madam, do you know?"

"Late next week, I believe."

Hilda, still at the top of the ladder, and Norah, clutching the drapery, looked at each other. Norah's face, usually bright with color, blanched.

"Madam," said Hilda hesitantly, "maybe—maybe it would be good to tell Mrs. Warren that—that you and Colonel George concern yourselves in this matter. I would be happy to take a message, madam. Mrs. Warren might like to know that the Studebakers . . ." She ran down. Even she couldn't add more embroidery to that thin tissue of an excuse. She looked pleadingly at Mrs. George, whose lips—surely they twitched slightly?

Hilda had no idea whether her substitute mistress knew about the events of last year, in which Hilda had established a bit of a reputation as a sleuth. Mr. Clem knew, and presumably Mrs. Clem, but Colonel and Mrs. George? The wealthy did not, as a rule, concern themselves much with the private lives of their servants. So long as they did their work, stayed out of trouble, and didn't indulge in the annoying habit of giving notice, they entered the thoughts of their employers about as often as the furniture they kept clean.

If Mrs. George had been amused, she showed no sign of it now. "That might be a very good idea, thank you, Hilda," she said gravely. "It may be some little comfort to the poor woman to know that we are taking an interest, and intend to make sure the right person is brought to justice. I shall write a note, and you can take it to Mrs. Warren before luncheon." She paused a moment, as if choosing her words carefully. "Don't feel obliged to hurry back, Hilda. Mrs. Warren may wish to talk to someone, and I understand you are very good at listening."

There was that suggestion of a twitch again. Hilda nodded submissively, but her eyes were dancing. Mrs. George knew! That might make things very much easier.

It was only about an hour later that Mr. Williams sought out Hilda. "You are to take this note to Mrs. Warren and wait for a reply. See you don't dillydally!"

"No, Mr. Williams." And what you don't know won't hurt you, Mr. Williams!

The weather continued hot, though clouds were gathering. Autumn in Indiana was a very changeable season. Hilda, as she hurried, in her hot uniform, wished it would change to proper fall weather.

Colfax Street, where Mrs. Warren lived, was just a block north of Washington, and was the same sort of elite neighborhood. The mayor, Schuyler Colfax Jr., lived there, along with many more of South Bend's notables. The Warren house, a large Queen Anne about twenty years old, was a block west of the mayor's and on the other side of the street. Hilda wondered idly who the original owners had been. Surely Mr. Warren had bought it recently, when he began to accumulate wealth. If Patrick's account was true, he hadn't been a rich man long enough to have built it.

It was lavishly turreted, with an elaborate roofline and a great deal of decorative woodwork picked out in a tasteful scheme of yellow and white and several different shades of green. It ought to have been a cheerful house, but now its closed blinds and the swath of black crepe on its front door proclaimed it a house of mourning. There was something mournful, too, about the weeds coming up through the bricks in the path and showing here and there in the flower beds. The whole house, in fact, was showing signs of neglect. Nothing obvious, but the stones of the foundation were missing some mortar here and there. The lattice under the porch was broken in a couple of places and needed painting in several more.

Perhaps Mr. Warren had lived here only a little while and had not yet had time to get the place in proper shape. Or perhaps, just perhaps, the fortunes of Roger Warren were not quite as healthy as it was supposed.

Hilda filed away that thought, climbed the porch, rang the bell, and waited.

There was no answer. She rang again.

From somewhere in the depths of the house she heard a faint cry. "Ingrid. *Ingrid!* Oh, where *is* the girl? She's never where she ought to—Ingrid! Don't stand there gawping, girl, answer the door!"

Hilda pretended she had heard nothing when Ingrid, her color high, opened the door.

"Good morning, Ingrid." She spoke in Swedish. "May I come in? I have a note from Mrs. Studebaker—Mrs. George Studebaker—to Mrs. Warren."

"I will give it to her."

"I am to wait for an answer."

"She has a caller."

"I will wait."

Somewhat reluctantly, Ingrid admitted her to the shadowy front hall.

"I am surprised," said Hilda, her face set disapprovingly, "that Mrs. Warren is accepting calls. Especially in the morning." Afternoon, as everyone knew, was the time for calls.

"Not a social call, business. It is Mr. Avery."

That was intriguing. Mr. Avery, calling on Mrs. Warren only a few days after she'd been widowed? Hilda remembered the smile the two had exchanged at the dinner party. Was it more significant than she had supposed?

"Oh?" she said, loading the monosyllable with innuendo.

"No, not that kind of business. Real business. Mr. Warren was to sell a piece of land to Mr. Avery, but he had not done it yet. So Mrs. Warren has completed the sale. Mr. Avery came for the deed, and to give her the money."

"Oh, but I thought . . ." Her voice trailed off. Her mind raced. "A great deal of money, do you think? Because," she went on carefully, "I am sure she needs money, with her husband gone, poor lady."

Ingrid snorted at that. "She wasted enough of it while he was alive, and she will probably waste this, too, no matter how much it is. Mr. Warren was a rich man, but look at the state of this house!"

"I saw that the gardener had not done his work properly."

"He is not given the time to do his work, nor the proper direction. And I—I was sent on errands every day. Go to the public library to exchange my books! Go to Solari's for some more chocolates! Go to Wyman's and see if the lace I ordered has come in! And then he would come home and scold her because the house had not been dusted and the groceries had not been ordered, and she would cry and say he did not give her enough money, and she needed more servants. And *she* would scold *me!* As if it were my fault that she sat and read novels and ate candy all day, and never—"

"Sshh!" The murmur of voices became louder as a door somewhere was opened. Footsteps sounded on a wood floor.

"Now, don't forget, dear lady. If there is ever any way that I can be of service to you, please call on me."

"Thank you, Mr. Avery. It is most kind, but I'm sure I'll be able to carry on, difficult though everything is. My sister will look after me."

"Are you certain you're wise to leave South Bend? A place, after all, where you have devoted friends." He pressed her hand, emphasizing his own devotion.

"I shall carry on," she repeated. "Ingrid! Mr. Avery's hat!"

Ingrid produced the hat. Mrs. Warren herself took his stick from the brass stand and handed it to him. Mr. Avery, with a courteous word to Hilda and Ingrid and a lingering smile for his hostess, finally allowed himself to be shown out. Mrs. Warren turned to Ingrid.

"And why are you standing here gossiping with this stupid girl? You ought to be packing my things!" And to Hilda: "What are you doing here, anyway? You ought not to have come to the front door."

"I came to deliver a note, madam. I was to wait for an answer," said Hilda. Her voice was icy. A servant on her mistress's business was admitted as the mistress would be, as this rude woman ought to know. Fuming silently, she handed over the expensive envelope with Mrs. George's monogram embossed on the flap.

Mrs. Warren's face turned a dull red, but she said nothing as she quickly read the note. "No answer," she said briefly when she had finished in the attic. "Or tell your mistress I hope they find the man who killed my husband, but I cannot bear to dwell on the matter. Ingrid, I wish that trunk to be ready for the expressmen this afternoon. Oh dear, oh dear, I am too ill to deal with all this just now!"

She allowed herself to droop, and made her languid way up the stairs.

"Is she really ill? Should you go to her?"

"There is nothing the matter with her that a slap in the face would not cure!" Ingrid spoke in a vehement whisper. "It was bad enough when Mr. Warren was alive, and she accused me of—of—"

"No!"

"And I never! He paid no attention to her because she was such a sorry bargain of a wife, not because he paid attentions to me. I would never, anyway. He was a cold, hard man, and if it is a sin to say that now that he is dead, then I am a sinner!"

"Ingrid, she spoke of a trunk. She goes to visit her sister?"

"She goes to stay with her sister. She plans to leave South Bend as soon as she can close up the house."

"But you will lose your job!"

Ingrid tossed her head. "I should have given notice long ago. I can find a better job, and she will give me a good reference."

"Will she? Are you sure?"

"Oh, yes. You saw how Mr. Avery acted! There are things I could tell . . . not that I suppose it means anything, really. He smiles at women to get what he wants. But she would not want it known. Oh, yes, she will give me a good reference!"

Hilda had been given so many things to think about that she

almost forgot the question she had most wanted to ask. She could not, now, ask Mrs. Warren, but Ingrid might know.

"Ingrid, did Mr. Warren talk, at home, about the thefts from the building site? You know about those?"

"Oh, yes, they talked. Very loud, they talked!"

"Do you think that Mr. Warren had any idea who the thief was?"

"Mrs. Warren asked him, just a few days before he was killed. I heard her, but he wouldn't answer. He said that she was not to worry, that he would take care of it. Myself, I thought he knew, and Mrs. Warren thought so, too. She begged him to go to the police and leave it to them. She might have known he would not listen to her. He never did. He said she was foolish, that they would never listen to him, that they would never believe it, unless he had proof."

"That they would never believe him? He said that?"

"Or something like that. He said, too, something odd. I had not thought of it until now. He said that he might be able to end the sabotage, even if he could not prove anything. 'I may find a way to put a stop to it.'" Ingrid quoted the phrase in English. "And when Mrs. Warren asked what he meant, he said it was better for her not to know, that it was a business matter."

"What else?"

"Nothing else. He did not want to talk about it, and when he was annoyed he could be very short with her. He got up and left the room, and I had to hurry to be away from the door when he came out."

Hilda nodded absently. If the two had been closer friends, Hilda might have warned her that listening at doors could lead to unexpected complications. As it was, she let it go. She needed everything Ingrid might learn in the next few days.

"And there was nothing else? No other conversation, at another time, no letters, or . . . ?"

But before Ingrid could reply, a voice floated down the stairs, high and petulant. "Ingrid!"

"I must go."

Hilda whispered one last question. "When does she leave town?"

"At the end of next week. Good-bye."

While Ingrid trudged wearily up the stairs, Hilda let herself out the door and started for home, a whole new set of speculations in her head.

17

In vino veritas. —Latin proverb

I F Hilda had learned anything from the near disaster of her first brush with murder a year and more before, it was to keep some of her thoughts to herself. So although her visit to the Warren house had caused a number of ideas to lodge in that busy mind, she made no mention of them to John Bolton when she stopped at the carriage house.

John's attitude toward her had changed. Whether because of a grudging respect for her or because he feared what she could divulge, he no longer, apparently, regarded her as a potential conquest. They would never, Hilda felt, be good friends, but they might be wary allies. It was in this capacity that she approached him.

"So where've you been, then, in the middle of a workin' day?"

"Mrs. George sent me on an errand to Mrs. Warren."

He looked at her sharply.

"Yes, I asked her to send me. Or if I did not quite ask her—oh, it does not matter, John. She knows what I try to do, and she will help me, but we do not talk about it. *Ja?*"

John shrugged and went back to grooming Star, one of the mares. Hilda got straight to the point.

"Did you talk yet to anyone?"

He shrugged again. "I've not had a chance to see Kovacz. Thought I might drop over there after supper. Had a word with

Sobieski, though, when I drove Colonel George to Oliver's this morning."

"What did he say?"

John patted Star's neck and shrugged again. "Not much. He doesn't know about any labor problems at Studebaker's, but he agrees something's going on. The men are all too closemouthed. He thinks maybe they're holdin' their fire till Mr. Clem comes home."

"But that is wicked! Mr. Clem, his health is better, but he is an old man. They should be ashamed to worry him."

"Yes, well . . ."

"And besides, he is good to his men. John, you know he is, no matter what you say sometimes. It is these other men who make you talk foolish. Mr. Clem, he will listen to his workers when they have troubles, he will even lend them money—"

"All right, all right, I *said* Sobieski didn't know of labor troubles there! Do you want to know what else he said, or do you want to do all the talkin', as usual?"

Hilda bit back a retort. "I wish to hear."

"You told me to ask about Warren, so I did. Sobieski didn't know nothin' about stealin' from the city hall site, nor about Warren's business at all, but he did say . . ."

His voice trailed off and he began combing Star's mane. Hilda nearly stamped her foot in impatience. "John! Tell me!"

"Seems to me you've turned a bit bossy lately, haven't you?"

She gritted her teeth. "John, I must go in. Mr. Williams will be angry. Tell me now: What did he say?"

"Oh, nothin' all that important. Only that there were rumors Warren had a bit of an eye for the ladies, and he wouldn't be surprised if Mrs. Warren was a trifle fed up, that's all. Oh, and he said Warren didn't seem to have quite so much money lately as he used to, or that's what he heard. Now, if you don't mind, my fine lady, I have to get Star hitched up. The landau's goin' out."

Mr. Williams was in a fit of nervous impatience when she reported back, and she had no chance even to organize her ideas for several hours. Colonel and Mrs. George lunched out, so the servants had a hasty meal and then went back to hard work.

They were all a little on edge. Would Mrs. Clem notice anything amiss? Had the house been allowed, in any way, to deteriorate in her absence? Was any ornament not where she preferred it to be? Had a rug been scuffed unduly, or a curtain frayed, or a plate chipped? No one could recall any domestic disasters, but Mr. Williams prowled the house unceasingly, checking for such things and irritating his underlings till they were ready to throw something at him.

Tired and harried, Hilda still managed to slip out of the house at five o'clock to meet Patrick. She was eager to hear the results of his bibulous search for knowledge.

It took him a little while to get to it. He was, Hilda observed, not looking his best. His eyes had lost their usual sparkle, and seemed to droop. His whole appearance, in fact, seemed to droop, and when Hilda greeted him with a cheery "Good afternoon," he winced.

"Would ye mind speakin' a little quieter?" he asked in a husky whisper. "An' could we move into the shade, please?"

"Why? The sun is not bright. And Mr. Williams will not hear us. He polishes the silver in the pantry and will—"

"Hilda, please!" Patrick's voice was anguished. Hilda stopped talking and surveyed him coolly.

"You were late to bed, *ja?*"

"Very."

"You drank much?"

His response to that was a muffled groan.

"Wait." She vanished into the house and returned with a small canvas bag.

"I have cracked some ice," she said softly. "Lean back, so, against the tree, and put this on your head. Then tell me quickly what you have to tell me and go home to your bed."

It was at times like these that Patrick remembered why he appreciated Hilda. He did as he was told and looked up at her quizzically. "Where did ye learn how to deal with a state like mine?"

"My brother," she said briefly. "In winter. Not often. Now

tell me, if you are well enough. Did you learn something?"

"I'd not be here if I hadn't, an' that you can believe."

"Patrick, I do not scold; you have punished yourself enough. But why did you drink so much? I wonder if you can even remember what people said."

He groaned again. "I didn't go for to do it! I started out nursin' beers, hardly had enough to take the edge off me thirst. But then someone came in with the news that Flynn was in jail, an' I was that upset, I started drinkin' in earnest."

"He is out of the jail now," Hilda said quickly, and explained about Colonel George's intervention.

"I know all that, an' more," said Patrick with some satisfaction. "He didn't bail Flynn out at all."

"But—"

Patrick held up his hand. "He got him out, all right, but on his own word. Colonel George's word, I mean. So we have to produce the real culprit, and soon—the colonel is countin' on us."

"Ah, so that is why Mrs. George—but tell me what you know so that you can go home."

He grinned weakly, moved the ice to an even sorer spot, and settled to his tale. "At first the talk was all about the president and the assassin. Have ye seen today's papers, by the way?"

She shook her head. "Mr. Williams ironed them and took them straight upstairs."

"The news is good. He's doin' even better. They're sayin' he can be moved to Washington soon."

"That is good, *ja*." She gave a sharp little nod.

"Well, the men were all sayin' last night that he'd recover, but that Czolgosz ought to be strung up, even so. I asked a question or two, but I couldn't get anybody to say anything good for the man. An' you'll understand, in company like that, I couldn't say anything meself, anything questionin' the government, like, fer fear I'd be strung up meself. But I didn't hear no talk about anarchy, nor about any troubles here in South Bend."

Hilda nodded. It was discouraging, but no more than she

had expected. The men who had attended Czolgosz's meeting would not now be eager to air their views, not unless they knew their company very well indeed.

"So in about the third place I went to, I finally got 'em to talkin' about the murders here. An' that's where I finally learned somethin', though I don't know if you'll think it's much."

"Anything is good, Patrick. I know so little."

"Well, ye know I told ye he wasn't well liked—Warren, I mean."

"You said his men, the men who worked for him, did not like him. And I told you that the businessmen did not like him."

"Yes, well, he was neither the one thing nor t'other, ye see. He'd pulled himself up by the bootstraps."

"The Studebakers did that. They were very poor when they came to South Bend. But everyone likes and respects them."

"Yes, but that was fifty years ago and more. They worked hard, they made pots of money, they got respectable and turned Republican and built mansions. They *acted* like rich people. Warren, he'd only been at it for ten years or so, and he made money, but he still acted like he was poor. Penny-pinchin', a Democrat—all that. So his men thought he was trying to lord it over 'em and keep 'em down, and the businessmen, people as rich as he was, and richer, thought he was an upstart. He didn't belong anywhere."

"That is sad, Patrick," said Hilda, her voice soft. "Not to belong."

"I thought so at first. Not anymore, not after last night."

"Why? What did you discover?"

"Mind, I don't know if it's gospel truth or not. They was all drinkin', an' they might've said things that were a bit—well, exaggerated. But if they were right, there was big trouble brewin' at the new city hall."

"Yes, yes, you have told me about the thefts, the destruction," said Hilda impatiently.

"It wasn't just that. The men were threatenin' to strike, and from the talk last night, they meant it. He was a slave driver, Warren, from what they said. Time was, he'd work as hard as any o' them, but that'd changed. He wasn't there most o' the time these past few weeks. An' when he was, his mind wasn't on the job. He'd give the men orders to do somethin' stupid. If they argued, he'd blow up; if they just went ahead an' did it, he'd flay 'em alive for doin' the work wrong. No matter what, they were wrong. An' he kept 'em workin' that week when it was so bl—bloomin' hot. One of 'em passed out, an' they all near walked off the job then.

"Hilda, there was some as fair hated him."

She thought about that and then gave one of her decisive nods. "This is good, Patrick. I mean, it is bad, and I am sorry your head hurts so much, but it is good that we know. The more we know, the sooner we can rescue Flynn from the danger his silliness has led him into."

"We hope," said Patrick, serious again.

"Yes, we hope. Patrick, we can do only our best! If that is not good enough . . ."

They looked at each other. Somewhere a dog began to bark, and Patrick put a hand to his head with a moan.

"You must go to bed, Patrick. You are not on duty tonight?"

"Not until tomorrow, saints be praised."

"Then rest."

"What're ye goin' to do, then?"

"I do not know yet, Patrick. I, too, have learned things, peculiar things. I do not yet know how to put them together. And I have little time even to think, for tomorrow Mr. and Mrs. Clem return."

"And high time, I'm thinkin'. He's needed here at home. Don't you work too hard, now."

Hilda hesitated, then threw caution to the winds, leaned over, and gave Patrick a kiss on the top of his head.

"Thank you, Patrick. I must go in!"

And she was gone almost before Patrick had time to be astonished.

18

WITHIN FOUR WEEKS
The President Will Be Fully Restored to Health
SAY PHYSICIANS TODAY
—headlines in South Bend *Times*, September 12, 1901

THAT night at bedtime Hilda and Norah had a chance to talk, for the first time since morning.

"Did you find out anything?" asked Norah as she dropped down into Hilda's chair with a heavy sigh.

"Yes, much, but I can make little sense of what I have learned. I must think hard. And you?"

"I asked first," said Norah stubbornly, pulling off her boots with a grunt.

Hilda, sitting on the bed, sighed and twisted around to unbutton her waist. "I learn that Mr. Avery is very nice to Mrs. Warren and has given her much money—"

"Oooh!"

"—much money for a piece of land he has bought—"

"Oh."

"—that Mr. and Mrs. Warren quarreled much, that Mrs. Warren is moving away from South Bend, that Mr. Warren maybe liked other ladies too much, that some of his workmen hated him, and that he knew who was stealing from the city hall."

"*Who?*"

"I do not know. He would tell no one. I said I could not make sense. Now you must tell."

"Well, I don't have a long string o' stuff like that—but then, *some* people didn't have Mrs. George's permission to go gaddin' about."

"*Ja, ja,* you know I gad about to save Flynn's neck! Go on." Hilda stood to take off her skirt.

"Well, I talked to Deirdre—Deirdre Moran, the new maid next door?"

Hilda nodded, stepping out of her petticoat. The Ford family had moved into the next house on Washington a couple of months before, and brought with them a large staff whom Hilda did not yet know well.

"She goes to St. Pat's, o' course, so I know her. Well, she was sweepin' the front porch, an' I just happened to be outside takin' a breath o' fresh air—"

"*Ja, ja.*" Hilda was tired and ready for sleep.

"So we got to talkin' about the rummage sale the church is havin' next week. You know we're doing' it with St. Stephen's, since they're a new parish and need money, and all the ladies have been collectin' the stuff for weeks. I help when I can, but—"

Hilda yawned openly and plumped back down on the bed; the springs creaked. "But what is this to do with the murders?"

"And aren't I tellin' you? So Deirdre, she was workin' yesterday at the church, it bein' her day off, with a girl named Marika Kovacz, from St. Stephen's."

"Kovacz! But that is one of the names—"

"Yes, and I asked, and he's her brother!"

Hilda had no trouble interpreting this remark. "Oh, but that is good, Norah! Kovacz, it is a common name here. There are many, many Hungarian families."

"Just a stroke o' luck," said Norah modestly. "But I latched on to it quick an' asked her all about the brother." She glanced at Hilda and decided teasing her with tidbits of information was not a good idea. "Hilda, I found out a lot! They're poor as poor, for one thing. The father's dead, like yours an' mine, only Mr. Kovacz died here in South Bend, a railroad accident two or three years ago. An' there's lots o' kids, the youngest but a babe o' three, I think she said, and the mother not strong, ill half the time."

She leaned over and rested her elbows on her knees, her chin propped in her hands. "But this is the part that's really interestin'. The brother—his name's Viktor—he's the only boy in the family, so he's the man o' the house now. An' ever since the father died, Deirdre says Marika told her, he's been gettin' stranger an' stranger. Cross, an' hot-tempered, like he never was before. Even goes around mutterin' to himself! An' Marika, she's worried sick about him."

Hilda's mind raced. "And he is poor, so he might hate the rich, and he is one of those who listened to the wild talk of Leon Czolgosz, and—oh—he worked for Mr. Warren! If he was one of the men who hated him—Patrick said—oh, Norah!"

Norah stood up, stifling a yawn. "An' if you're thinkin' what I think you're thinkin', then explain to me this: If they're so poor, and Viktor the only one earnin' anything much, why'd he do himself out of a job by killin' his boss? Just you tell me that, Mr. Pinkerton."

"Oh. Oh, you are right, but . . ." She pulled the pins out of her hair. Heavy braids fell to her shoulders. "Who is Mr. Pinkerton?"

Norah laughed and opened the door. "Ask a policeman! An' when I start gettin' silly, I'm too tired to think straight. I'm goin' to bed." She stepped into the hall, then put her head back around the door. "I'll never forget what you done for Flynn, Hildy. When I say me prayers tonight . . ." She lifted a rosary from her pocket and blinked back a tear or two. "We'll come up with some answers in the morning."

But the next day catastrophe struck.

It began before breakfast with the arrival of the butcher's boy, who arrived dripping from the steady drizzle that had set in. He brought bacon, pork chops, three dressed chickens, a huge sirloin of beef, and news.

It spread through the great house like a thick gray fog, blanketing everyone with gloom and despair.

"The president is dying!"

Hilda heard one of the dailies call the news to Norah. She herself was in the drawing room putting last-minute touches on a huge arrangement of dahlias and chrysanthemums. She sucked in her breath, allowed a dahlia to fall to the floor, scattering scarlet petals and drops of water on the polished wood, and ran to the servants' room in the basement.

Mrs. Sullivan was sobbing. Mr. Williams stood, stone-faced, in front of the fireplace, wringing his hands.

"What is it? What has happened?"

"We know but little, Hilda. I have sent Anton to the *Tribune* office to learn what he can. We have merely the word of the boy from Sindlinger's that the president's condition began to worsen in the middle of the night, and the end may be near."

When Anton returned, there was a little more hope. The president had evidently been unable to tolerate the solid food he had been given on Thursday, small though the amount had been. He had experienced violent digestive upsets during the night, so much so that the effect on his heart was feared. The latest bulletin, however, was that he felt somewhat better and his heart seemed a little stronger.

The household had no time to fret. Mr. and Mrs. Clem would be home very soon. They went about their duties with heavy hearts, jumping nervously every time a delivery boy came to the back door, straining their ears for the cries of newsboys with an extra edition.

The morning passed. Norah and Hilda didn't even try to talk privately; they had no heart for it. Private trouble, even trouble as grave as an accusation of murder, paled before the great national affliction. They finished their cleaning, served Colonel and Mrs. George their lunch, and took a hasty one themselves with the other servants. Then Mr. Williams, resplendent in his best morning coat, drove with John to the Lake Shore and Michigan Southern depot to meet the master and mistress.

All the Studebaker whistles had been scheduled to blow as the train pulled into the depot. Hilda heard them as she hurried into a clean uniform just after one-thirty. She must look her best, as the house was looking its best. Oh, how she wished Mr.

and Mrs. Clem had returned the day before, when the president seemed to be doing so well, and there could have been unrestrained celebration. Instead there must be gloom, worry, and solemnity.

Mr. Clem was one of the president's most ardent supporters. He had contributed generously to the 1896 campaign and had tirelessly delivered speeches on Mr. McKinley's behalf. He would be devastated by the news.

And when Mr. Clem was devastated, Mrs. Clem was distraught.

The servants lined up in the great hall to greet the returning travelers. They looked tired, Hilda thought, but Mr. Clem had a better color than when he had left, and more spring in his step. It looked as though the trip had been good for him. But what would the death of the president—if the worst did happen—what would that do to Mr. Clem?

The world seemed filled with trouble and tragedy.

After the travelers were given a light meal and their personal servants had put them to bed for a restorative nap, Hilda had a chance to talk to Michelle, the ladies' maid who had made the trip with her employers.

"How does he feel?" was her first question. Michelle had no doubt what she meant.

"He was feeling very much better until we reached New York. But when he fell—you have heard about his fall, yes?"

Hilda nodded.

"He was not hurt, not badly, but it is not good for a man his age to fall. And it upset him, in his mind, *savez-vous?* It made him afraid, and that also is not good. He is seventy. He has the right to a quiet, peaceful old age. But I am afraid . . ."

Hilda did not press her to continue, for she was seized by sudden panic. He could not die! Not Mr. Clem! There was too much death in the air—but not Mr. Clem! He had been somewhat ill for a long time, but old people are prone to minor illnesses. It meant nothing. He was home now, and Mrs. Clem would look after him with the dedication she had always shown.

But he must not be upset. Michelle was right. Emotional up-
heavals were bad for him.

And everything was going wrong! Trouble at the Studebaker
plant, the murders at City Hall, the president failing . . .

"Does he know about the president?"

"*Mais oui*, of course! There were papers at every station
along the way. He is very unhappy, but he has known about the
shooting since it happened, so he is not shocked, I think. It is
shock that is so bad."

"I hope Tommy will take good care of him."

"He is a good, devoted valet, even if he is a colored man. He
will tend to him, but , , ,"

Again the thought was left unfinished.

Patrick did not come to report that day, nor did Hilda expect
him. All the attention in the house was focused on a bedside in
Buffalo, New York. The gala meal Mrs. Sullivan had planned for
the homecoming, and for Mr. and Mrs. Clem's thirty-seventh
wedding anniversary, was modified to plain meat and potatoes,
and even that was left half uneaten as the inhabitants of the
great house waited uneasily for news to break. Everyone, mas-
ters and servants, went to bed early, exhausted by nervous antic-
ipation.

It was two-thirty in the morning when the news came. Hilda
woke to the solemn tolling of the courthouse bell, and tears
began to slide down her face. The newsboys, fanning out from
the *Times* building, shouted their headlines in voices that broke
more than once.

"The president is dead! Extra, extra! Death of President Mc-
Kinley!"

19

AMERICAN PEOPLE BOWED IN DEEPEST MOURNING
DEVIL'S OWN DEED
Has Its Consummation In The Death of the Nation's
Honored Chief
—headlines in South Bend *Times*, September 14, 1901

THE household, on Saturday morning, was in disarray. Normal work was suspended. Between tearful readings and rereadings of the newspaper accounts, the residents of the house tried to put it and themselves into proper mourning. Black crepe was purchased in quantity, dressmakers and milliners were summoned, flowers set out so gaily to welcome the Studebakers home were quietly thrown away and vases full of black plumes put in their places.

All over town flags were being lowered to half-mast. Portraits of the president, draped in black, appeared in store windows and in parlors of rich and poor alike. The business of South Bend ground to a halt, and foot and horse traffic was sparse and muffled as the city grieved.

Despite the best efforts of his wife and Tommy Nowlin, his valet, to make him rest, Mr. Clem insisted on getting up that day. It was disrespectful to the president's memory to loll in bed all day. There were jobs to be done, plans to be made. As the town's most important Republican, perhaps excepting the mayor (who was, after all, the son of the late vice president Schuyler Colfax and entitled to some preeminence), he felt obliged to take a leading role in the memorial arrangements for the fallen president. His health? Pah! He felt fine.

Hilda crept about her duties like a pale shadow. Her eyes were swollen with weeping. She had never been a Republican. There was a Swedish McKinley club in South Bend, and the Studebaker brothers actively encouraged its activities, but Hilda, a woman, could not have joined, and, in any case, her sentiments were with the Democrats. But she had respected and revered the president, and had gloried in working for someone who knew the highest official in the land, someone who had given him a fine carriage, who had his ear in any emergency. The president had felt just a little like family. And now he was gone, and the president was Theodore Roosevelt, a flamboyant character whom many Republicans feared and disliked. Even the sky seemed to mourn, with lowering clouds that brooded and sulked and refused to rain. Everything was awful.

The local murders, of such importance only a few days before, had been relegated to the back pages of the newspapers, but while Hilda was tidying the library she saw one item that made her feel even worse.

"The trial will be on Friday," she said to Norah as they set the luncheon table together.

"I know. Flynn stopped by to see how I was gettin' on and told me."

"It is not much time, especially—"

"I know," said Norah again. There didn't seem to be anything else to say.

Patrick made a brief visit at five o'clock. Hilda had forgotten to watch for him, but she was on the front porch with Anton, draping crepe on the massive front doors, when Patrick walked around from the back and found her.

At the sight of him, solid, reliable, a good friend, Hilda burst into fresh tears.

"Now, then, don't cry," he said in his warm, sensible voice, and Hilda cried the harder.

"Ye look a sight, ye know," he observed. "Your nose is red an' your eyes are all puffy."

She was too upset even to lose her temper. "I know," she

said, sniffling. "I do not care. Patrick, what will happen to us all?"

Anton paused on his ladder, a length of crepe in his hand, to hear what Patrick would say. He, too, was fearful. Nothing so terrible had ever happened in his young life, and he had not believed that such a thing *could* happen in America, land of his parents' dreams.

"Now, don't you fret, girl," said Patrick with a stout confidence that was perhaps somewhat more robust than his actual feelings. "Nothin' bad's goin' to happen. It's an awful thing, sure, an' we're all sad as we can be. But it's not the end of the world, not here. We've a new president an' the government'll go on, same as always. There are those who might have their quarrels with it now and again, me for one, but it's a good government taken all in all, an' a great country, an' it'll carry us through."

The front door opened. Mrs. Clem stood in the doorway, nodding approvingly. "You're a sensible young man, whoever you are," she said. "If you've come to call, we are not receiving visitors, I'm afraid. You've done that very well, Hilda, Anton. Excuse me." She walked regally down the steps and on down the drive, Hilda curtsying in her wake.

"I have to go," Patrick whispered. "I only wanted to see you were all right. Tomorrow afternoon?"

"I do not know, Patrick. Nothing is the same now."

"I'll be here. If ye're not, I'll know why." He took himself off the same way he had come—the back drive for tradesmen, servants, and their callers.

The rest of the day went by in a kind of nightmare. Hilda did what she was told and nothing else. Her head seemed empty, echoing with the bells that had filled the air all day with their mournful tolling. The president is dead. The president is dead. There was no reality in life but that one dreadful fact.

The dressmakers had not had time to finish mourning clothes for the family, let alone the servants, but the milliners had made heroic efforts and come up with mourning bonnets for all. Sunday morning Hilda dressed in her black uniform skirt and waist, pulled on the black bonnet with its thick veil without a thought to whether it became her or not, and trudged off to church, for once heartily thankful for the chance to meditate and pray. If ever there was a time for prayer, it was now.

The church service was a somber one and the social gathering afterward very subdued. Hilda spoke for a moment to the Lindahls. Ingrid was indignant.

"She gives me no time to grieve. I, too, am sorry about the president, but I cannot go home and be with my family. Packing, taking things down from the attic, answering the bell—"

"Callers?" Hilda was truly shocked.

"Well, one caller. One of the men who worked for Mr. Warren. She would not see him, but it was I who had to tell him so." And more of the same.

Nor was the family meal the usual festive affair. Gudrun's cooking was as good as ever, her fruit soup as delectable, her coffee as fragrant, but little was eaten and less was said.

Hilda was ready to leave almost as soon as she had helped clear the table and wash the dishes. "I am sorry," she said, taking off her apron and standing in the kitchen doorway, "but I am too sad to talk, and so are you all."

"A better day next week, little chick," said Sven, patting her shoulder.

His sympathy gave her sudden resolve. "Sven," she whispered with a glance at her sisters, still putting the dishes away, "may I talk with you? Alone?"

His face filled with alarm. "There is something the matter? You are not ill, or—"

"No, nothing at all. I simply wish to talk to you. Without the others hearing."

"Very well." He raised his voice. "Gudrun, Freya, I will walk Hilda home. I will not be long."

When they were well away from the house, Hilda took a deep breath. "Sven, you will maybe be angry, but I have heard things that disturb me, even more now that the president is dead."

"Rest his poor soul," said Sven. "What have you heard, little chick?"

"I will tell you, and I will even tell you what I have told no one else. I will tell you from whom I heard these things."

Briefly she related the overheard conversation and Colonel George's remarks.

"You should not have been listening," said Sven severely.

"I know, and I am sorry. I wish I had not heard, but I did, and Sven, I am afraid. Will you tell me what he meant?"

They had walked most of another block before he replied.

"I cannot tell you, Hilda. I am not angry. I am sorry I lost my temper last Sunday, but things had been—difficult. I understand your concern, and it does you credit, but I have made a solemn promise, and I will not break it. I will tell you not to worry too much."

"But if there is danger . . ."

Sven paused again, as if to choose his words carefully. "It is possible that there is danger of a certain kind, but I do not think the risk of it is very great. More than that I cannot say. I must return, Hilda, or Gudrun will worry. Try not to be too unhappy, little one."

Hilda knew no more than before, and she was less reassured than confused.

Having spent so little time with her family, she arrived home before Patrick came to call. She would not walk out with him, she decided. The weather was sullen, not a day for outdoor enjoyment, and it would not, anyway, be appropriate on this day of all days. She would sit on the bench and wait for him, talk with him a little, and then spend the rest of the day . . .

How would she spend it? She had gotten into the habit of seeing Patrick. Norah would be with her own family, worrying about Flynn, or else over at St. Patrick's, finishing preparations for the rummage sale, if they were still going to hold it. Michelle—well, she and Michelle worked together well enough, but they weren't close friends. Her other friends, the servants who worked nearby, would be . . . she didn't know where they would be. She had never inquired what they did with their Sundays. There was always Patrick.

She had always argued when one of her sisters, or Norah, intimated that Hilda and Patrick were growing too close. She would continue to argue with them, because it wasn't in her nature to admit she was wrong. But . . .

At that uncomfortable spot in her musings, Patrick came up the back drive, not whistling as usual, but quietly, gravely.

"So you're here."

"Yes. But we cannot—"

"I know."

Silence.

"I thought you might be off somewhere, tryin' to find out somethin' or other."

"Patrick! I could not, not today."

"Are you givin' it up, then?"

"No! Of course not, I—" She stopped, confused. Did she plan to continue? Could she go about asking questions, perhaps dangerous questions, with the president lying dead?

Could she *not* continue, with Flynn's trial only five days away, and the frenzy against anarchists likely to be redoubled?

"I do not know, Patrick," she said, forced to be honest with him and herself. "It—it seems wrong to ask about these things now, but also it seems wrong to do nothing. There is more danger now, I think, for—for anyone who might have said too much, and the wrong things."

"Yes, I'm thinkin' you're right about that." He looked at her steadily, his face a mask. "Danger also for anyone who pokes their nose in."

Was that why she was reluctant? Was she afraid?

"Oh, Patrick, tell me what to do!"

"An' that I'll not do, me girl. You've your own mind to make up, haven't you?"

She felt as though she had been thrown into deep, cold water without a lifeline. She actually gasped at the shock, though she instantly suppressed the sound and hoped Patrick had thought it was a sneeze.

Ever since Hilda had known Patrick, her attitudes, her actions, had been hammered out in opposition to his ideas of what she ought to be and do. Now that, for once, she wanted his guidance, he was refusing to oppose her, refusing to offer his opinion at all.

She could think of nothing at all to say.

Patrick sat down next to her. "I saw Flynn today at mass," he said conversationally. "He'll likely lose his job, you know, for fightin', if nothin' else."

Hilda looked at the toes of her boots, which needed brushing, and was silent.

"I talked to Lefkowicz, too. He says the police are pantin' to get the trial over and done with, so they can forget about the whole thing."

She looked up at him.

"Well, I'll be goin', since it's no day for a girl to go for a pleasure walk. Be seein' you."

He trudged down the back drive with never a backward glance.

Hilda took a very deep breath, let it out in a gusty sigh, and stood up. There was only one thing for her to do. She had known for two days that she had to do it, but the death of the president had knocked the sense out of her head. Patrick had restored it.

She set out to find the Kovacz family.

20

The ladies of St. Patrick's church will have a rummage sale corner Chapin street and commencing Monday, the 16th, and continuing a week. We solicit the aid of friends who have clothing, furniture, etc., to donate to drop a postal to St. Patrick's rectory; will send for them.
— South Bend *Times*, September 9, 1901

S HE didn't know where they lived, but Norah might know. Or somebody at St. Stephen's.

She went first to St. Patrick's, and struck it lucky. Dozens of people swarmed about the church, some carrying armloads of clothing and household goods, some stacking the goods into wagons, some standing and giving orders and pointing and generally getting in the way.

She saw Norah almost immediately. She was one of those who were working hard, and she was glad of a chance to rest for a moment.

"You still hold the sale, then? Even with the president . . . ?"

"It's for the poor. The president'd not mind that, now would he? They'll get good, warm clothes for the winter at a cheap price, an' we'll maybe get enough money to finish repairin' the roof and give some to St. Stephen's, too. It's no insult to the president's memory!"

"No, I suppose not. But—you talk of the poor—I must see Marika Kovacz. Or her brother," Hilda added doubtfully. She wasn't sure she was ready yet to meet someone as strange as Viktor was reported to be.

Norah jerked her head. "Marika's inside somewhere, helpin' with a little last-minute sortin'. An' Viktor was here, but I think he's gone with the other men with a load."

"Gone to where?"

"Chapin Street. The sale's to be on the corner o' Chapin and Jefferson. There's more traffic there than in front o' the church, ye see."

Hilda relaxed a little. Chapin Street was two long blocks away. She could delay her meeting with Viktor for a little while. "How does Marika look?"

"Tired an' worried. Oh, you mean what does she look like? Short, dark. Today she's wearin' black, o' course—there, that's her, just comin' out the door with that pile o' clothes." She pointed.

Hilda saw a girl who would have been very pretty if she had not been so thin, if the frown on her face had been a smile. Her black hair, where it had worked loose from her fringed black scarf, curled around a face whose pink cheeks had faded. Her feet, Hilda felt, were meant to dance. Just now they plodded. She was carrying much too heavy a load.

That gave Hilda the opportunity she wanted. The large stack of goods Marika was carrying began to slide, and Hilda ran forward and caught a worn, much darned blue cap as it was about to fall to the sidewalk. She couldn't imagine anyone buying it. It was frayed and faded, and though an attempt had been made to clean it, it still smelled of hair oil.

"Thank you." Marika extended two fingers from the bottom of the bundle. "I will take it now."

"I can carry it to the wagon," said Hilda firmly, and helped herself as well to two or three shirts from the top of the stack.

Marika said nothing.

"I am a friend to Norah Murphy," said Hilda. "Do you know her? She is a member of St. Patrick's."

"I attend St. Stephen's."

Hilda contained her impatient sigh. "But Norah knows you, even if you do not know her. She told me you are Marika Kovacz. I am Hilda Johansson. I am happy to meet you."

They had reached the wagon and disposed of their burdens. Hilda put out her hand, and Marika had little choice but to shake it.

"I think your brother knows another friend, John Bolton?"

That brought a response, at last. Marika looked at Hilda with hostility in her dark eyes. "You are a friend to John Bolton?"

Hilda didn't miss the look. "Not perhaps a friend. I know him. He is the coachman where I work."

"Oh. Tippecanoe Place."

She didn't say any more. She didn't have to. Her voice dripped with bitterness. The staff at Tippecanoe Place had the best servants' jobs in town, and every other servant (except perhaps those working for the Olivers) knew it and envied them.

This time Hilda's sigh could not be hidden. "Miss Kovacz, Norah has told me of the troubles in your family. My father, he also is dead. I understand how bad this can be. If you would like a yob—a job—at Tippecanoe Place, I can maybe—"

"I have a job. I work for Mrs. Avery. I have no need of your charity!"

Mrs. Avery! This was luck! A chance, maybe, to get into the Avery house, to find out more about that purchase of property from Mrs. Warren, about Mr. Avery's feelings for her . . . Hilda swallowed her temper and her retort. "I am sorry. I did not mean to sound . . . Miss Kovacz, my mistress is in need of another good maid. It is you who would be charitable if you would come." She crossed her fingers behind her back.

Marika shrugged. "Maybe another time. I do not wish to change jobs now. If you know so much about my family, you know that my brother—"

"What about your brother?" The man who had come up behind them was an older version of Marika, but his good looks had survived better. His short-cropped hair curled in unruly fashion all around his cap; his face was sunburned. He was tall while she was slight, but there could be no doubt that he was Viktor.

"I was going to say, that you had lost your job." Marika's look at her brother was meaningful; what it meant, Hilda unfortunately had no idea.

"For now, I have lost my job. But they will hire another contractor for the city hall, and I can work for him as well. And better!" he added fiercely, raising a bandaged hand to push his hair away from his brow. He was wearing no coat or tie, just a white shirt nearly as thin and worn as the flannel ones Marika was finally giving away.

"Viktor, your hand!"

The bandage, somewhat dirty, showed a few red spots.

"Oh, Marika, do not fuss! I scraped it, setting up the table, and it started to bleed again a little. It is all right." He pushed back his hair again; again it evaded the discipline of his pomade and fell over his brow. Hilda found the effect rather attractive.

Viktor's eye caught hers; she let her eyelids droop demurely.

Viktor did not look away. "Marika, where are your manners? You have not introduced me to your friend."

Marika had turned away to the wagon and was making herself very busy with the bundles of clothing. Hilda looked up at Viktor, put out her hand, and introduced herself.

Viktor gave her his left hand. "I cut myself on the job," he explained, holding up the bandaged right hand. It was red and scaly above the bandage and looked to Hilda as if it needed medical attention. She had opened her mouth to say so when he went on, "Your name is a familiar one, Miss Johansson. You are in service at Tippecanoe Place?"

"Yes. John Bolton has maybe talked to you about me."

"Ah, that is it! You are—you are the housemaid." Somehow the end of the sentence didn't seem to go with the beginning. Hilda wondered what he had meant to say.

"I have tried to persuade your sister to come and work with me, Mr. Kovacz. She would earn more, I think, and it is not a bad place to work."

Marika opened her mouth, but Viktor forestalled her. "It is kind of you, Miss Johansson, but I hope that soon my sister will not need a job at all. If things work out as I have planned, there will be enough money." He smiled, showing a good many very white teeth. "Do not worry about us."

Marika looked again as if she would speak. Viktor shook his head. "We spend too much time talking," he said firmly. "There is Mother, needing some help, Marika. Please excuse us, Miss Johansson."

"I will help you," Hilda began, but brother and sister had turned away to hurry back into the church.

Hilda hesitated. She very much wanted to continue the conversation, but a Swedish Lutheran did not readily enter a Catholic church. She stood, irresolute.

"Learn anythin', did ye?"

Norah had materialized at her side.

Hilda turned her eyes heavenward. "I do not know. They said things, yes, but . . . I must talk more with them."

"Well, the blessed Lord knows there's enough to do here, if ye want to stay and help. Ye can help carry those curtains, for a start. That fool boy's about to drop 'em."

But though Hilda stayed and worked for an hour, she had no further opportunity to speak with either Marika or Viktor. She fetched and carried. She overcame her scruples to go in as far as the church basement (which really didn't count, she reasoned). She found one old calico wrapper she thought might be useful and talked Norah into letting her take it on the spot, with promise of payment—five cents as soon as she got home to her purse. She even rode with one wagonload to the site of the sale and helped unload. There was not a Kovacz to be seen.

It was almost, she thought when she had given up and was trudging home, as if they had been avoiding her. But why would that be? Viktor had been attracted to her at first; of that she was sure. She was pretty enough to have had admirers. She knew an appreciative look when one was directed her way. But when he'd found out who she was, he had taken no more interest.

She stopped in at the carriage house when she got back to the Studebaker property. John was sitting in front of the stable, half asleep. "Sit down. You look tired. And a little dusty, if you don't mind my saying so."

"I am dusty, and I must change my clothes. I will not sit, thank you, John. I wish only some information."

John sighed. "Can't you let it alone just for a day or two? It's Sunday!"

"It is also five days before Flynn's trial," she said coldly. "No, I cannot leave it." She was perhaps the more vehement, having considered that very course of action only a few hours before.

"I wish only to know what you told Viktor Kovacz about me."

"Kovacz? About you? Why would I talk to him about you?"

"I do not know. He said that you did. Also, he acted very peculiar when he said it."

"Well, I—oh! I might've told him you were—" He stopped. Hilda waited.

A tinge of red colored John's sun-browned neck and spread to his face. "I said to someone, and it might've been Viktor, that you—umm—liked to ask questions and—umm—find out things."

"I see. You told him that I was a—a snoop!"

John took a deep breath. "And if I did? Aren't you?"

She struggled. Rage and pride fought against curiosity and the need to clear Flynn. Curiosity won, by a narrow margin.

"Then you will not be surprised that I ask questions. There is one more. How did Mr. Kovacz hurt his hand?"

"Hurt his hand? Which hand? I didn't know he had."

"He wore a bandage on his right hand today. It was dirty; he has worn it, I think, for some time."

John shook his head. "He didn't have one on Saturday night when I last saw him. The night of the murder. I'd have noticed."

"So he lied," Hilda said, almost to himself.

"Lied about what? Here, what's this all about?"

"Now who is a snoop?" said Hilda, and walked resolutely to the house.

The afternoon was nearly gone, but Norah had not yet returned. Listlessly, Hilda went to her room and exchanged her heavy black clothing for the wrapper she had just bought. As she was hanging her waist on its hook in the wardrobe she saw the feed sack lying forgotten in the corner.

She had promised to wash and iron the flag, and she had forgotten all about it. Her fine deduction about the time of the murder had proved useless; there was no reason now not to go ahead with the chore. She took the sorry banner out of the sack and shook loose the red, white, and blue folds, wrinkling her nose as she did so. Really, it did smell!

Then she smacked her forehead and sniffed again, deliberately this time. Mud. Mildew, probably. Blood, certainly. And that faint, sweet smell . . .

There was a stain near the middle of the flag that she had overlooked. She studied it now. An oily stain. She held it up to her nose.

Hair oil. Unless she was very much mistaken, the same hair oil she had smelled only a couple of hours before.

Viktor Kovacz's.

Viktor, with an injured hand.

Viktor, who had worked for Mr. Warren and had been acting very odd and had met with the assassin Leon Czolgosz and—

She sat down on the bed, hard. Had she, a few hours before, met and talked with a murderer?

21

There are worse things than a lie . . .
— Anthony Trollope, *Doctor Wolfe's School,* 1879

YOU go too fast, she said to herself. You do not use your mind. Think!

What had Norah said? That Viktor would not kill his employer, because then he would have no work. That was sensible.

Yes, but today he had said he had plans, that Marika might not need a job.

Why was his hair oil on the flag?

It might not be his. Many men might use that same brand. Men with little money, thought Hilda. It was cheap, strong-smelling stuff. She brightened at another thought. She did not know that the cap she had picked up was Viktor's. Marika might have brought out a load of things someone else had donated. Surely the family did not have enough money to give away things of their own.

But he had lied about his hand. He said he hurt it on the job, and that could not be. His job ended on the Saturday, because Mr. Warren was killed that night, and no more work has been done at the city hall since then. And his hand was not hurt Saturday night. John had said so.

Her thoughts thrashed around like a rat in a trap, seeking a way out.

The fact was, she didn't want it to be Viktor.

Trying hard to be honest, she considered why not. She

didn't know him. She had only just met him, and he had been rather rude, if anything.

But only, she reminded herself, after he knew who she was. Before that he had been interested in her.

So is that what it is? she asked herself scornfully. You are flattered and do not wish to think bad things of him?

That was certainly part of it. She admitted it. A girl likes to be admired. She does not like to think that her admirer might be a murderer.

It went deeper than that, though. Viktor was one of her own kind, an immigrant, working hard to try to better himself and support his family in this new, sometimes cruel country. Like her, he had to fight prejudice and bigotry. Like her, he had to work at low-paying jobs and struggle for recognition of his true worth.

She had been lucky. She had a better job than most of her fellow servants, and a far, far better home. The servants' quarters at Tippecanoe Place were more comfortable than any worker's house, and the food was certainly superior. Didn't she have a responsibility to those less fortunate than she?

Poor Mr. Lefkowicz was an immigrant, too, she thought grimly. And he is dead. If it was Viktor Kovacz who killed him . . .

Without conscious volition, she found herself getting back into her clothes and descending the narrow back stairs once more, in search of John Bolton and information.

John hadn't moved, except to tilt his chair back against the stable wall, the better to nap. It was that sort of afternoon, slow and heavy. Hilda wished she could go back upstairs and nap herself, but she knew her conscience wouldn't let her.

"John," she said tentatively.

Maybe he wouldn't wake up. Maybe she could wait until later . . .

But her soft greeting brought a responsive whinny from one of the horses within, and that brought John out of his doze. His chair tilted forward; the front legs struck the ground with a thud.

John yawned, stretched, and laid his head to one side. "Now what?"

"You were sleeping . . . I should not bother you . . . I will come back another time. . . ."

He shook his head. "Sit down, and tell me what it is you want."

She sat, looked down, and bit her lip. "I wish to know . . ." There was no help for it. She took a deep breath. "John, you said that Flynn Murphy was the last one to leave your meeting the night of the murder. When did Viktor Kovacz leave?"

Maybe he wouldn't remember. Maybe he would say Viktor left just before Flynn did.

"It's funny you should ask that. Because I was just thinkin', myself. Wonderin', you know, how he hurt his hand."

They looked at each other. John was as reluctant to speak as Hilda to hear him, but he finally came out with it.

"He left first, Hilda. He'd been edgy all the evening, impatient, nervous—I'm not sure what to call it. We were all on edge, mind you, worried about what might happen, but Viktor acted like he had something else on his mind. And when that first little rumble of thunder sounded, he said he had something to do at home before the rain came, and he was up and out of here. He didn't even finish his beer."

Hilda moistened her dry lips. "How long was it, after he left, before the rain did come?"

"I wasn't lookin' at the clock. But we all talked for a little longer, and had another drink, and then Sobieski and Kapinski left and Flynn stayed on for a little . . . I'd say it was a good half hour. Maybe longer."

"And you had been drinking. My brother, he says sometimes then time passes by more quickly than you think."

"That's true." A silence grew, stretched, thickened.

It was John who said it at last. "The city hall's no more than ten minutes away."

"Oh, no, John, it is six blocks. Fifteen minutes to walk, at least!"

"Kovacz is tall. He has long legs."

Hilda thought about that, and sighed. "John, what did you talk of that night? You, Flynn, Viktor, the others? Did Viktor—did he speak of Mr. Warren?"

"Not as I recall. Mostly we talked about the pickle we were in, and how we were going to get out of it. Kapinski talked some about the automobiles going to Buffalo, I recollect. He's dead set against automobiles, thinks they're a curse, going to take the bread out of the workingman's mouth." He laughed humorlessly. "I forget just why, now. Kovacz, he mostly paced the floor. Didn't say much."

Hilda could make no sense out of that, but as she tried to think what other questions to ask, they heard the crunch of gravel, the creak of harness leather. "That'll be them, comin' home," he said unnecessarily. He stood, heavily, and moved toward the porte cochere to assist his employers, all four of them, from the carriage of the friends with whom they had taken a Sunday afternoon drive.

Hilda stayed where she was and watched them alight and enter the house, her mind elsewhere. What was she to do?

Flynn's life was in danger. If he were convicted of murder, the penalty was death. He didn't do it, and a judge and jury might believe that, but he had been spreading radical ideas. Loudly and fervently he had been spreading them, and the public was in no mood right now to give any firebrand the benefit of the doubt.

More frightening, the matter might not even come to trial. Already in the newspapers some people were suggesting that Leon Czolgosz should be lynched. If public opinion in South Bend were aroused . . .

She wouldn't think about that terrifying possibility. She needed to act, not frighten herself into paralysis. She stood, squared her shoulders, and made for the house.

She must do it immediately, for dusk was falling. The ladies would want to rest after their drive, and then they would be busy changing for dinner. They would probably be upstairs already.

She all but ran up the flight of narrow back stairs, pausing to straighten her skirts and pat her hair into place before walking down the hall and tapping lightly at Mrs. George's door.

"Michelle? Come in." The voice sounded slightly impatient. A well-trained ladies' maid did not knock on doors.

"It is not Michelle, madam. It is Hilda. I am sorry to disturb you. May I speak to you, madam?"

"Oh, Hilda, you're not going to give us notice? With Mr. Clem so tired, and all of us upset about the president? I'm sure, if it's a question of wages—"

"No, no, madam, I would not do such a t'ing! I have come only to ask for a little time away from work. A day, two, three maybe . . ."

Mrs. George's eyes narrowed. "Is someone in your family ill, Hilda?"

"No, madam."

"I see."

Hilda thought she probably did. She stood her ground and waited.

"If you want time off, Hilda, you should go to Mrs. Clem. Now that she has returned, she is your mistress."

"Yes, madam." Hilda didn't stir.

Mrs. George sighed. "Very well. I don't want to know what you're up to. I believe I'd better not give you a vacation, but if you should find you need to be away from the house rather more often than usual, I'll see to it that no one interferes, neither your master and mistress, nor Mr. Williams. Your work must be done, of course. I'm sure you understand that."

"Yes, madam. Thank you, madam." She curtsied and turned to go.

"You're not happy about this, are you, Hilda?"

Hilda hesitated in the doorway. "No, madam. I do not like some of the things I think. But I cannot—I cannot stand by and watch a bad thing happen."

"Then I wish you well in your efforts. Send Michelle to me, will you?"

Hilda was dismissed.

22

We . . . recommend a young man to . . . remember that no one acts with a due regard to his own happiness who lays aside, when married, those gratifying attentions which he was ever ready to pay the lady of his love. . . .
—Richard A. Wells, *Manners Culture and Dress,* 1891

S HE could do nothing that evening, she told herself. Tomorrow would be soon enough. She picked at her supper and went straight up to her room afterward, pleading a headache so she wouldn't have to talk to Norah. She didn't want to talk to anyone.

After a restless, troubled night, the headache was real enough. Nevertheless, she rose before the alarm rang. There was work to be done, a day's work in half the day. Then she could put it off no longer. She would have to do her real duty.

Despite the brilliant sunshine and cool weather—autumn behaving as it should, for once—she went about her work with set face and tightly closed lips, and Norah and the other servants left her alone. Hilda, for all her temper, seldom went about in a sustained bad mood. When she did, however, they knew she was to be avoided.

She took a moment, in her lightning pass through the library, to look up Kovacz in the City Directory and note down Viktor's address. He would probably be at home. He had no work just now. If he wasn't, she would just have to seek him out. She had thought about it all night, and had decided she couldn't turn him over to the police without talking to him. Maybe there was an explanation.

Maybe he really was the murderer, and he would kill her, too.

She'd worry about that when the time came. What could he do in broad daylight, after all?

She would neither ask Mr. Williams for permission, nor tell him she was leaving. Mrs. George had promised to make things right. She might tell John where she was going. Just in case . . .

She pressed her lips together even harder and gave a vicious swipe at a lamp, nearly upsetting it with her dust rag.

Lunchtime would be good. He would almost certainly be home then. Her own lunch could wait. She wasn't hungry anyway.

The farrier was at work in the stable when she went to find John. She let him finish nailing a shoe onto one of Star's hooves before she spoke. Star was a nervous horse who hated having her feet messed with; Hilda didn't want to startle her.

"Where is John, Mr. Garrity?"

"Upstairs, cleanin' up. Say, have you heard the news?"

"No. I must speak to John—"

"You haven't heard about the murder?"

The world reeled. She couldn't catch her breath. She stumbled.

"Here, sit down before you fall down! Are you all right, miss?"

"I—yes. Who—what—?"

The stairs clattered with the sound of heavy boots.

"Hilda! I was just washing my face so I could come in and tell you, gentlelike. Did this fool—?" John glared at the farrier.

"John, I am all right. Tell me! Who has died?"

"Mrs. Warren, just this morning. Here, where you goin'?"

She was halfway down the back drive before he got out of the stable.

That was what came of putting things off. She ought to have gone last night, gone straight to the police. Now someone else had died! And Ingrid—she began to run. *Was Ingrid hurt?*

The Warren house wasn't far away. Hilda arrived, breath-less, her hat askew, and rang the bell.

There was no answer. She rang again and peered through the big oval window in the door. The blinds had been raised, the black crepe removed. She could clearly see into a sunny hall, a hall bare except for the tall blue jar in one corner, a lone, bat-tered walking stick in it. She could see into the drawing room beyond and a little way up the stairs. The house was utterly still; not a dust mote stirred in the shafts of sunlight.

"What do you want, girl?"

Hilda whirled around. An elderly woman stood on the side-walk, stiff and stern.

"You'd better be off. There's nothing there for you."

"I look for my friend. She is the maid here. I want to know she is all right!"

"Oh, so you've heard the news, have you? Terrible thing, ter-rible! I don't know what the world's coming to, when respectable folks can be murdered in their own home, and in the middle of the morning, too. And none of us neighbors knowing a thing about it till that maid comes out, screeching like a locomotive. No discipline, you young people!"

"Yes, but Ingrid—she is not hurt?"

"Never heard anybody bad hurt who could yell that way! She's gone home, girl, and you'd best do the same. Who knows where that murdering monster is now? Could be lurking around here, for all we know. You go on home."

Hilda had no intention of going home. She knew where the Lindahls lived, near the Swedish Church. She wasted no time getting there.

She found Ingrid ensconced on the parlor sofa, the center of a flock of friends and relatives, all clucking anxiously. Forcing her way through the crowd, she fixed Ingrid with her eye and de-manded, "What happened? Tell me!"

Perhaps it was the strangled urgency of those few Swedish words. Perhaps it was the desperation in that cold blue eye. The crowd of women quieted and looked at Hilda, who waited, taut as a telegraph wire, for Ingrid to answer.

Ingrid had never seen Hilda like this. She had the sense not to indulge in hysterics. "I found her," she said. "She was in the drawing room, and her head . . ."

Her voice trailed off into a half sob. Ingrid's mother bustled forward with a protest. Hilda ignored her.

"When? When did you find her?"

"Midmorning. About nine. I was nearly ready for a cup of coffee, but I had to ask her a question about the big blue jar in the hall, which she had made me carry down all the way from the attic, so I—"

"Yes, yes. Did you hear nothing?"

"No. I was in the attic all the morning, going through old things, sorting what to pack for the movers and what to throw away. And it was so hot there under the roof! I opened all the windows to let in the cool air, and it was noisy outside. Carriages, you know, and the birds, and the cicadas—"

"But someone must have come! Did no one ring the bell?"

"Mrs. Warren said she would answer the door until I had finished in the attic. She wanted me to hurry. She wants to leave—she wanted to leave South Bend as soon as she could."

Ingrid threatened to cry again. Hilda hurried on. "But you would have heard the bell if it rang?"

"Oh, yes, I heard it ring. I know who it was, too, and I told the police."

Hilda thought her heart would batter its way out of her chest. "Who?" she managed to whisper.

"I saw him when he left, because he slammed the door and I heard it and I looked out the attic window." Ingrid stopped there to sniffle. Hilda could have slapped her.

"Who?" she asked again.

"That man who came before, one of the city hall laborers. Kowal, I think his name is."

Somehow Hilda got herself out of there. She found herself passing the church and, on impulse, opened the door and went in.

She sat down in a back pew, struggling with her thoughts. Kowal? Kovacz, almost certainly. If she had gone to the police yesterday with her suspicions of Viktor Kovacz, Mrs. Warren would still be alive. It was her fault.

No longer did she wish to speak to him. He had killed three people, one of them a woman. She wished only to see him behind bars where he could do no more harm. The only way she could expiate her own guilt was to give Viktor over to the police as soon as possible, before they arrested some hapless man named Koval. She breathed a prayer for forgiveness and for the grace to do what she had to do, and left the church.

Her way to the police station led her through the Hungarian neighborhood, past, she realized as she looked at the house numbers, the Kovacz home. At the sight of it her heart filled with pity, despite her fear. So small a house for so large a family! It was tidy, it had a scrubbed look, but it badly needed paint, and the roof was missing a shingle here and there.

As Hilda looked, the door opened and a small, frail woman came out, the toddler in her arms wailing listlessly. She looked anxiously up and down the street, saw Hilda, and hurried to the gate. "Excuse, please?" she said in heavily accented English. "I look for my son. You have seen him? You know him, I think. My son Viktor?"

Hilda was not at her best just then. She simply stood and looked at the woman.

"Excuse for speaking to you, but I am Mrs. Kovacz. I see you yesterday at the church. You speak to my son."

"Oh. Yes. Yes, I have met your son, Mrs. Kovacz." Her throat nearly closed with the ache of compassion. What could she say to this poor woman?

She was still talking. ". . . this morning, and he says he will be in for his dinner, and I have not seen him, and I think, maybe you, you know him, maybe you know where he is."

The words finally penetrated. "Viktor is not here?"

"No, and I do not know where he is, and I cannot leave. Alexa, this little one, she is sick, and—"

"I will try to find him for you, Mrs. Kovacz!"

Perhaps he was in the hands of the police already. But no! Why would they suspect him? They knew nothing of the meeting, nothing of the flag, of Viktor's burned hand. . . . Marika! Marika would know where he was. Brother and sister were close. He would have gone to her after . . . afterward, for help and advice. And Marika would be at work. Where did the Averys live?

She had called there once, a year or two ago, to deliver an invitation from the Studebakers. It was on Colfax, she was sure. On the same side of the street as the mayor's house. A block away? Two blocks?

She flew past the rummage sale on Chapin without even seeing it, turned east on Colfax without looking at the progress of the fine new Methodist church Mr. Clem was building, and then began to walk more slowly. It was along here somewhere. Was that it, the tall red brick?

It was the third house she tried, a large, ugly, impressive fieldstone house rather like a baby Tippecanoe Place. The back door was open; she knocked on the screen and someone called, "Come in! You've been long enough about it!"

The small hallway was dark, but she knew her way around a service wing and found the kitchen with no trouble. The cook stood by the scrubbed oak table, hands on hips.

"You're not the boy from Nickel's!" she said accusingly.

"No. I must speak to Marika. Where is she, please?"

"How'd I know? I know I can't make a cake for tea without those raisins, and where are they?"

Hilda slipped out of the kitchen. After a moment of hesitation in the hall, she pushed on the swinging door that separated the backstairs premises from the rest of the house.

She had no right whatever to be prowling around someone else's house, but she had to speak to Marika. She had to know where Viktor was.

She paused to listen. The house was very quiet. Maybe Mr. and Mrs. Avery were out. They didn't seem to be in the dining room, and it was lunchtime, wasn't it? Or maybe it was later than that. She couldn't remember. Her head was light and her stomach sore, but whether from hunger or worry, she didn't know.

There was no one on the main floor. Drawing room, front parlor, music room, dining room, study, front hall. She swallowed hard. Dared she go upstairs?

The front screen door banged. Panic-stricken, Hilda saw a shadow cross the green marble of the entryway. And steps began to descend the stairs. Someone coming from both directions. She was trapped!

There was a door under the stairs. Praying that the stair cupboard wasn't packed as tightly as most, Hilda silently opened the door and squeezed inside.

It was a tight fit. The cupboard *was* crammed full, of winter woolens, probably. The smell of camphor was suffocating. She pushed herself as far into the scratchy folds as she could and, with her fingernails on the latch, brought the door to. She dared not try to close it; there was no knob on the inside.

Two sets of footsteps on the stairs over her head, one following the other.

"That will do, Marika. I don't know what you were doing in the attic, and I don't care. Under no circumstances are you to sneak around like that again, do you understand?"

Marika murmured something Hilda couldn't quite hear.

"All right, now go on about your business. I want that entry floor cleaned thoroughly, mind you. The workmen left it dirty when they put it in. Hello, darling, what are you doing home at this time of the day?"

"I came to see you, my dear." There was an interval of not-quite-silence. Hilda found herself hot all over and glad she couldn't see outside her prison. Then Mr. Avery spoke again, his voice lowered this time, presumably because of Marika in the entryway.

"I've brought some news, actually. Mrs. Warren was killed this morning."

"Herbert!"

"Yes, quite a shock, isn't it? Someone has it in for that family. That Irishman they arrested—I was against them letting him out on bail, and now it looks as though I was right. I never told you, but I thought I saw him skulking around the place that day I went to close the deal on that property."

Mrs. Avery spoke, so softly Hilda had to strain to hear it. "What a pity he didn't kill her before you gave her the money."

Hilda was shocked.

"Now, now, my dear. I'm only glad I was able to make her happy for a little while. I'll always remember that last time I saw her, poor thing—standing squinting into the sun in that impossible front hall, bawling at her maid to get me my hat. She couldn't wait to get me out of there, now she had the money. Even handed me my stick. I must say, I was as anxious to leave as she to get rid of me. I nearly kicked over that ridiculous blue vase, or whatever it was, in my hurry."

"Herbert! I thought you were fond of her. You certainly made eyes at her often enough."

"Oh, I was sorry for her, that's all. It must have been a dreary sort of life, married to that cold fish."

Mrs. Avery laughed softly then and said something Hilda was very glad she could not hear. The tone of voice was embarrassing enough, and Mr. Avery's, when he replied, was even worse.

When she heard two pairs of footsteps over her head, rapidly climbing the stairs, she could feel her cheeks burn. And what made it even worse was that she must follow them.

23

Ye have heard that it was said by them of old time, Thou shalt not kill, and whosoever shall kill shall be in danger of the Judgment; But I say unto you, That whosoever is angry with his brother without a cause shall be in danger of the Judgment. . . .

—The Gospel according to Matthew

IT was a tricky maneuver. Hilda didn't know exactly where Marika was, nor how long it would take her to polish the entryway. It was small, but cleaning a marble floor was a demanding business. If Marika had to make up the cleaning powder, of soda, pumice, and chalk, she'd be busy in the scullery for some time. If not, she'd be back immediately, but her attention would be fully occupied. Could she, Hilda, slip up the stairs unnoticed?

For she now knew where Viktor was, and she now wanted passionately to talk to him.

Ever so cautiously, she eased open the cupboard door. It was a great relief to be able to breathe air uncontaminated by camphor. Through the small crack she had created, she could just see the door open into the entryway. She could not see Marika, but she couldn't be far away. Her heart beating wildly, Hilda opened the door all the way, praying it wouldn't squeak.

It didn't. Marika, or someone, had greased the hinges properly. The hall carpet was thick, as was that on the stairs. Carefully keeping to the wall side of the steps, as less likely to creak, she climbed, expecting every moment to hear an outcry.

When she reached the landing and the turn, out of sight from below, she leaned against the wall and took several deep breaths. She felt as faint as though she had climbed a mountain. But she couldn't stop there, for now she could be seen from above. She was reasonably sure the master and mistress of the house would not come into the hall and see her. She tried not to dwell on why not. A fine thing, for a respectable man in the middle of the day! At any rate, it was with his wife, which made it better, she supposed. Though no decent woman would . . .

She firmly halted that train of thought. A decent woman wouldn't speculate on activities behind a closed bedroom door. An unmarried woman ought not even to know about such things, but servants acquired an education early.

Her concern now ought to be not what her betters were up to, but what other servants might be in the house to catch her, and how she was going to find the attic door. She could hardly try every door in turn!

Her position was a vulnerable one. She had to get off those stairs. Tiptoeing, and blessing Mr. Avery for buying good carpets, she ascended the last few steps and darted down the hall to its end. Her fright was beginning to recede and let her mind work again.

The back stairs would be beyond that door, if she had the layout of the house worked out properly. And that, probably, would be where she would find the attic stairs as well—if there were attic stairs, and not just one of those pull-down ladders. Unfortunately, the backstairs region was also where she was most likely to encounter one of the servants.

Well, she couldn't stay where she was. Gingerly, she turned the knob and pushed open the door, peered around it, and whisked herself through.

Sure enough, narrow stairs led upward. They were, of course, bare wood. Hilda wished she could take off her boots, but without a button hook it would take too long. Stepping as silently as she could, she began to ascend the stairs.

These were not as well constructed as the main stairs. They creaked. At every sound Hilda froze, certain she would be discovered, but eventually she found herself at the top, facing the attic door.

She took a deep breath and opened it—and found herself nose to nose with Viktor Kovacz.

"You! I thought you were Marika! What—why—"

"Hush!" said Hilda. "Whisper, only. And we must not move about. They will hear us, below. Sit on that trunk, Mr. Kovacz. I must talk to you."

His eyes moved to the door behind her. Silently, she pushed it shut and leaned against it.

"Mr. Kovacz, I think you have not killed anyone, but you are in very bad danger. You must not leave this place, not yet. And you must answer my questions. Now sit!"

His jaw set, his eyes as mutinous as a small boy's, he sat.

A silence fell. In the hot, dry air of the attic, dust motes drifted idly in a slanting ray of sunlight. Viktor's tension fairly simmered.

Hilda crouched in front of him, her face close to his so that she could be heard. "Why did you cover Mr. Warren with the flag?"

He gasped. "How did you know?"

She relaxed a little. "I was not sure. There was hair oil on it. I thought it was yours. How did it get there?"

Why had she asked that? It scarcely mattered, but she wanted to know.

"It was windy. It was just before the storm, and the wind had come up. The flag billowed so, the easiest way to carry it was to wrap it around myself."

"But why did you want it? It was a foolish thing to do. And why were you there?"

The mutinous look returned.

"Viktor, I must know! I do not want to believe you are guilty, but I must know if I am to learn who did do these murders."

Suddenly he gave way. He groaned and put his head in his hands. Slowly, a bit at a time, it all came out.

"I went there to kill Mr. Warren." Hilda drew in her breath sharply, but Viktor went on, unheeding. "I admit that. It was very wrong, but I was mad, I think. There was no money, and my mother was ill, and—"

"Yes, that I know. But why would you kill the man who paid your wages?"

"She offered me money to do it. So much money . . ."

He nearly broke down at that, and Hilda had time to absorb the shock.

"Mr. Kovacz! Who offered you money?"

But she was already sure of the answer, and it was no surprise when Viktor, his voice muffled by his hands, answered, "Mrs. Warren."

That was apparently the worst part. He was able to go on more calmly. "I hated him, Miss Johansson. I will not deny that. He was a hard man. The other men all knew, and somehow she must have learned how I felt. She sent me a message that I was to visit her.

"I had never met her, and I was uneasy, but I went. I could not refuse a summons from my employer's wife. She was—she acted very strange. She told me that her husband was not kind to her, that he saw other women. Me, I thought she was imagining that part, but she believed it. And she said she knew I did not like him, and that he treated his men badly, and—and in the end she offered me a hundred dollars to kill him."

A hundred dollars! That was a great deal of money.

"And I agreed," said Viktor bitterly. "And I have not been able to sleep since."

He stopped. His jaw worked. Hilda would not let herself sympathize. If this man was not a murderer in actual fact, he was in spirit. He had been ready to kill. "Go on."

"There had been thefts from the building site—"

"Yes, I know about that."

"And he hired a night watchman. But when nothing happened, he decided to watch himself, with Lefkowicz, the foreman. Mrs. Warren, she tried to make him tell the police, but he was unkind to her and would not listen. It was then, I think, when he made her so unhappy, once more, that she decided . . . anyway, she did not know about Lefkowicz watching with him that night. She told me he would be alone, and I thought it was my chance. I meant to go as soon as it was dark, but there was that meeting, and I dared not stay away."

"John has told me that your nerves were bad that night."

"I just wanted to get it finished and be done with it! And when I heard the thunder and knew it would storm, I went a little mad. Somehow it seemed that, if I did not do it that night, there would never be another chance. So I left the meeting, and I ran, all the way, for I feared that he would leave. And when I got there—"

He paused, and Hilda waited, holding her breath.

"Miss Johansson, when I got there, there was a flash of lightning, and I could see him. He lay there on the ground, so still. I went to him, and he—he was dead."

Hilda released her breath and asked again the question that had puzzled her from the start. "And the flag? Mr. Kovacz, *why* did you cover him with the flag?"

Viktor ducked his head in an odd motion of embarrassment. "You will say this makes no sense, but he lay there, dead and helpless, and I—I had hated him, but now—and the rain was coming . . ." He shuddered. "The flag, it was blowing about on the porch of the stables next door. I saw it, and went and grabbed it, just before it blew away, and covered him. I could not just let him lie there in the rain."

"But you could leave Mr. Lefkowicz?" Hilda's voice was hard.

"I did not see him! It was dark, and I was afraid, and I did not know he was to be there. He was—he was my friend, Miss Johansson. I would have tried to help him, but I did not know!"

His voice had risen. Hilda put a finger to her lips, but absently. So that was all it was. No conspiracy, no hidden meaning. For a week she had looked for a link, and there was no link. The flag was a shroud, that was all.

She sighed. "I must go soon, Mr. Kovacz. First, show me your hand."

Wordlessly he held it out. Hilda gently pulled down the bandage and looked at the blisters, beginning now to heal. "That is a burn, not a cut. The fire at the stables?"

He nodded. "I do not know why you ask me questions. You know everything."

"I do not know, but I *think* you went back to the stables on Monday to find the flag. You thought it might be dangerous to you. You did not know the police had kept it. And it was night, and your candle touched off the straw."

He nodded again. "I tried to put it out. That is how I burned my hand. I had nearly succeeded when I heard the fire wagon coming, and I left quickly."

"I wonder," said Hilda thoughtfully, "who sent in the alarm. But it does not matter now."

"Miss Johansson, I must tell you—I—I followed you that night. I could not see your face—the night was dark—but I saw where you went. I had heard you talking with Mr. Cavanaugh, at the fire station, and—I was afraid, I . . ."

"And outside the carriage house—when John thought he saw someone?"

Viktor nodded. "I went to—to—I would not have harmed you, I wanted only—but you were with John, and again I could not see you properly, only your back, with John there."

Hilda clicked her tongue. "You have done many very foolish things, Mr. Kovacz. Tell me one thing more and I will go. What happened this morning?"

He bowed his head again. "I went to Mrs. Warren. I had gone once before, but she would not see me. I went to—I thought . . ."

Hilda shook her head sadly. "You went for your money."

"Yes, I did! Her husband was dead. That was what she wanted. What did it matter who killed him? She thought it was I, and I needed the money, and she did not. I knew she had enough money, for Marika had told me Mr. Avery had at last bought that land he had wanted so badly."

"Did she give it to you?"

"She did not. She told me she would turn me over to the police. She said she had never asked me to kill her husband. She lied—she spoke to me as if—she treated me like—"

"But you did not kill her." Hilda's voice was calm and sure.

"No, I did not. I shouted at her. I threatened her. I pleaded with her. But when I left she was alive, and I do not know who killed her."

"Yet you ran to Marika."

"When I heard that Mrs. Warren was dead, I was afraid someone might have seen or heard us, and they would think—"

"Someone did see you, and they do think. But I, I know that you did not kill. You almost did a very wicked thing, but the Herre Gud, he protected you from yourself. Viktor, you must now do a hard thing, to make up for your wickedness. You must go to the police and tell them everything."

"But I cannot do that! They will not believe me! They will—"

"No, they will not believe you. They will put you in jail. That, you deserve for making a bargain with the devil. And it is the only way that we will catch the real killer."

He groaned. "I do not know who the real killer is."

"I think I know, but I do not yet know why, and I can prove nothing. I must think of a plan. Wait, now, until the house is quiet. Do not go to your home, and do not tell Marika what you plan to do. But after she is gone from here, go downstairs very quietly, and leave the house, and go to the police station. You will not be in jail for a long time, I promise you."

And with the utmost stealth, Hilda crept down long flights of stairs, let herself out the back door, and ran all the way back to Tippecanoe Place.

24

O conspiracy! Sham'st thou to show thy dangerous brow by
night, When evils are most free?
—William Shakespeare, *Julius Caesar*

ILDA carried no watch. The cheapest ladies' watch from
Sears, Roebuck & Co. cost nearly three dollars, far too
much for the likes of her. She didn't usually need one.
She had grown up in the country, and was adept at judging the
time by the sky. This afternoon had been upsetting, however,
and her judgment—in that and other things—was unreliable.
She thought it was far later than in fact it was, and was surprised
when Mr. Williams was not lying in wrathful wait for her.

The only thing he said to her, when he encountered her in
the drawing room a half hour later, was, "Oh, Hilda, there you
are. You were not down for lunch. I trust you had a good rest.
You are not ill?"

"No, I—only I had the headache, Mr. Williams," she improvised rapidly. "I feel better now." For a minor illness that would
send her to bed might be very handy later.

"You are having too many of these headaches," he said severely. "You should see an oculist."

"Yes, Mr. Williams." She scuttled away to catch up on her
work.

As she worked, she thought, and as she thought, she berated
herself. She had been a fool. She had worried about anarchists,
and there were no anarchists—or if there were, she corrected
herself, they weren't involved in her problems. The murder of

Mr. Warren was somehow a private thing, and she was very close to knowing exactly how it had happened. Mr. Lefkowicz —well, he had been in the wrong place at the wrong time. And Mrs. Warren? That, too, she thought she now understood.

And what about Studebaker's? asked an uneasy corner of her mind.

Well—well, about that she would worry later. Just now she had to plan. There were still a few things puzzling her, and before she acted, she meant to know all the answers. She had very little time. Viktor would be in the hands of the police before the evening was over; the news would be in the papers tomorrow afternoon. Given the mood of the town, it might not be safe for him to remain in jail for long. And then, of course, Flynn's trial—if ever he came to trial, with the police otherwise occupied—was set for Friday.

There was one way to acquire a good many of her answers, and quickly, but it was very risky. She thought all afternoon, but try as she might, she could come up with nothing better.

So before she went down to the supper for which she was ravenous, she slipped into Mrs. George's sitting room, opened her dainty little desk, and helped herself to a sheet of writing paper, one of those thick, embossed envelopes, and a pencil. Her heart was beating fast as she slipped them into her pocket. This was the most audacious thing she had done yet. If it worked, though . . .

She waited until the servants' meal was over. Hungry as she was, she had made herself pick at her food. She rose from the table, stumbled a little as she pushed in her chair, and leaned heavily on it. She gave Mr. Williams a piteous look.

"Please, sir, I do not feel well. My headache, it has come back. May I go to my room and finish my work later?"

He sniffed, but she was well caught up with her work; he could hardly criticize. "Don't make a habit of this sort of thing, Hilda."

"No, sir." Norah opened her mouth to speak. Hilda frowned at her and made the most minute of motions with her head. Norah closed her mouth again. Hilda prayed that she understood, but there was no time to talk to her privately.

She trudged up the back stairs, but only as far as the main floor. Then she was past Mr. Clem's study and out the porte cochere door as fast as her feet could carry her.

The family was visiting the other Studebaker brother, Mr. J.M., planning some of the details of the McKinley memorial service that would be held on Thursday. They would be out for some time, and the porte cochere door would not be locked until they returned. If she returned after that—well, she would find a way to get back in. Or she would stay out until morning. The weather was chilly, but dry; she could manage.

When she was far enough away from the house to feel safe, she stopped and took her illicit stationery and the pencil from her pocket. Supporting the paper on someone's broad porch railing, she wrote a few words on it, slipped it into the envelope, and tucked in the flap. Then she crossed the street and, a few doors down, walked up to the house and rang the bell.

The butler who answered the door knew her, of course. He looked startled to see her at this hour of the evening, and calling at the front door.

"Good evening, Mr. Higgins. I have a note for Mr. Oliver. If he is at home, I am to wait for an answer."

The butler frowned. "He is at home, but he is going out soon. I will see if he has time to deal with the matter."

He took the note, frowned slightly to see that it bore no address, and looked at Hilda sharply.

She smiled innocently.

He shook his head. "Wait here."

She was left cooling her heels in the hall for what seemed like an hour, but was really about five minutes, before the butler returned, his frown more in evidence. "Mr. Oliver wishes to speak with you. Come this way."

Hilda was shown into the study, but with scant formality. She stood just inside the door, very much ill at ease.

"Sit down, girl!" It was an order, not an invitation. Hilda chose the least comfortable-looking chair and sat on the extreme edge of it. "That will do, Higgins."

The butler left noiselessly and closed the door behind him.

Mr. Oliver had very bushy white eyebrows and very black eyes. He directed them in a piercing glare at Hilda.

"Now, young woman, what's this all about? You've wangled your way in here under false pretenses. 'I wish for you to see and speak with Miss Johansson.' I presume you wrote this silly thing yourself?"

She nodded, unable to speak. She had seen Mr. Oliver many times when he visited at Tippecanoe Place, and she had always been afraid of him. He had a brusque manner and a quick temper, and he was, after the Studebakers, the most important man in town.

"And you stole your employer's notepaper to write it on."

"Yes, sir," she whispered.

"Very well. I let you come in here because I was curious. You have five minutes to prove to me that you have a good reason for this impertinence."

As artistic a liar as she could be, she knew this was a moment for the unembroidered truth. She took a deep breath.

"I came to you, sir, because I need some information about the city hall, and I think you are the only one who can tell me."

"What do you mean, you need information? Why?"

"To tell you that will take longer than five minutes, sir, but—oh, please, sir! It may mean a man's life!"

Oliver sat stolidly in his chair, offering her no help. Hilda swallowed hard and went on.

"I think, sir, that the trouble in town, the murders, that they are not the work of anarchists. I know that is what the police think, and that is what I thought at first, but I was wrong. I know now—well, I think—that they all join together in the city hall." She frowned. "That is not the right word. I do not know the right word in English, but your city hall is very important, sir, to learn what has happened."

She hesitated.

The snapping black eyes bored into her. "And that's why you wanted to talk to me. It's my city hall."

"Yes, sir." She returned his gaze candidly. Maidenly modesty would not soften this man, either.

"You tricked your way in here, young woman."

"Yes, sir. I did not think you would see me if you knew what I wanted. You would think I was yoost silly and stupid."

The mispronunciation was the first sign of her nerves. She bit her lip, but dared not go back and correct herself.

"I see. Well, if I'd thought that, I daresay I'd have been mistaken. Ask your questions."

She sat up even straighter. "Thank you, sir. First, I do not understand about the thefts and the destruction. You know about that, Mr. Oliver?"

"I do."

"Why would someone wish to do such things?"

"Ah, well, I've given a good deal of thought to that, though I can't say I've come up with much. Warren and I talked when it first began to happen. I was concerned, because it was causing delays, and I want this project to be finished on time. I'd promised Warren a nice bonus if it was, too, and of course he was worried he was going to lose it if much more went wrong. That's why he went to the site that night, I believe. Fool thing to do, but he wanted that bonus and he was determined to catch the fellow who was as good as taking it away from him."

"You would not—you did not think that Mr. Warren was at fault? You would not have taken the work away from him and given it to someone else?"

"Couldn't do that, young woman. Don't you know anything about contracts? Not unless he flat fell down on the job, and he wasn't doing that, not by a long shot. He was working as hard as he could, and working his men hard, too, day and night, good weather and bad. But he paid them a fair wage. They had no cause to complain." His tone was uncompromising. Hilda decided it would be wise not to argue the point.

"Mr. Warren, did he lose money because of the delay?"

"Not so far. He had insurance on the project, of course, so he lost nothing on materials or vandalism. Nothing except time, but if he lost too much of that, he'd lose the bonus. Not his fault, so far as I could see, but I keep to my word and I expected him to do the same."

Hilda thought hard. "Could he—if he stole the materials himself, and the insurance company paid, then he could return the materials and keep the money . . ."

Mr. Oliver barked a sharp laugh. "Think insurance men were born yesterday, do you? They made sure those materials were really missing, and more ordered, before they paid a cent, you can be sure of that. I know those men, and they personally made certain Warren was dead, and not by his own hand, before they'd write the check for his *life* insurance. They wouldn't be fooled by a shabby trick. They didn't get to be where they are without being careful.

"Anyway, missy, do you think I'd hire a man with that sort of character to build my city hall? Roger Warren wouldn't have pulled a trick like that. He was a hard man, and demanding, and I didn't much care for his politics, but he was honest. I'll have a hard time of it, finding another man to do the job I want, and it's apt to cost me money, what with the delays and all. Men won't want to work on the building now, and any contractor I find will likely have to pay a little more to get good men."

"So the only one who has lost because of the troubles is you, sir, *ja?*"

"I'd say," he said, looking at her from under his shaggy brows, "Roger Warren and his foreman lost a good deal, wouldn't you? And Mrs. Warren. And before you ask, no, I've no idea who was responsible for her death. A coward's trick, killing a woman, that's all I have to say.

"Now, then, I said I'd give you five minutes and I've given you fifteen. You'd better run home now before Williams catches you out. I'll wager he'd not approve."

"No, sir." She lowered her eyes demurely, but Mr. Oliver was shrewd.

"Did he forbid you to come?"

"No, sir. He did not know I was to come here."

"And that's not the whole truth, either. No, never mind. It's none of my business." He paused for a moment. "Do I remember some talk that you had a hand in unraveling that nasty business in the Harper family, a year or so ago?"

"I do not know what you have heard, sir," she answered carefully.

Again that bark of a laugh. "Keeping your own counsel, eh? Well, you seem bright enough. You've asked me more than the fool police did, at any rate. Not that it's been any use, that I can see, but you never know. Get along home with you, now, and I promise I won't tell any tales. But don't get in the habit of stealing your mistress's stationery."

Hilda wasn't sure, but she thought she heard him chuckle as she left the room.

25

... it is stupidity rather than courage to refuse to recognize
danger when it is close upon you.
        Sir Arthur Conan Doyle, "The Final Problem"

S HE hadn't been gone long. The porte cochere door was not
yet locked; evidently, the family had not returned. She
managed to slip inside and get up to her room without
being observed, and once there she flopped down on her bed.
She'd been given enough time to recover from a headache. Very
well, she'd make this a long headache and take some of that time
to think.

Small, isolated pieces of knowledge floated in and out of her
consciousness. A blue jar in a sunny front hall. ". . . made sure
he was dead before they'd pay his life insurance." An angry man
at a dinner party, his hand gripping his wife's arm. Marilta,
cleaning a floor.

She knew, now. She knew everything. What was she to do
about it?

"No one will believe me." Mr. Warren's words, but Hilda's
thoughts. There was still no proof. She would have to set a trap.

And she'd have to be quick about it.

There were still chores to be done. Hilda poured cold water
from the washstand jug into the bowl, splashed it on her face,
and ran downstairs to finish up before she got scolded.

If only John Bolton would come into the house! But he almost never did after he'd eaten his supper, and he did not tonight. Very well, she would have to go out to him. "Norah, I will

hang out the dish towels. The air will do good to my head." She had whisked out the door before Norah could question or protest.

The clothesline was near the carriage house. She hung up the towels hastily and then knocked on the stable door. There was no answer, so she opened it and went to the foot of the stairs leading to John's room.

"John! It is me, Hilda. John, come down!"

She dared not shout. The night was pleasant; the windows of the great house were open. She waited, then repeated her call.

This time he heard her and came to the head of the stairs.

"What is it now? Do they want to go out again, this late? What're you whispering for?"

"Sshh! Do not talk so loud. I must talk to you. Come down."

"You could come up, you know, anytime you've a mind to," said John wickedly, with a return of his old manner. But he came down. "All right, what's so all-fired important that you have to get a man out of his comfort at this hour?"

"I need your help, John. I have a plan."

John groaned and sat down on the bottom step, while Hilda quickly outlined what he was to do.

"You don't want much, do you?" he said when she had finished. "What if they don't want to come?"

"Tell them it is a matter of Flynn's life! They will come, I think, John. I think they like a fight!"

He grinned at that. "All right, if I can manage it—me and Murphy and Kapinski and Sobieski. At Warren's house in two hours."

"No later!" she said, and ran back to the house.

There was another half hour's work to be done before she could go upstairs for the night, and then she had to tell Norah what was planned. Norah was dubious.

"One o' these days you're goin' to go too far, and then you'll find yourself out of a job, or worse!"

"I know, Norah, but what else can I do? There is little risk, really. I am sure the murderer will go to the Warren house for the money."

"If you're right about who it is."

"I am right. I am sure. And with four men to capture the criminal, what can happen? Then they will take the murderer to the police, to be charged with breaking into the house, and the proof of the other things can come later. It will work, Norah."

Norah protested, but her heart wasn't in it. If this was what Hilda thought she had to do to free Flynn from suspicion once and for all, then she, Norah, would do her part.

"So I'm to let you out and lock the door after, and put up the chain, and then wait for you to come home. How long will you be?"

"I do not know. If the criminal is wise, the wait will be long. Me, I would not break into a house until the middle of the night. But who is to say if a wicked and impatient person will be wise? You do not need to stay awake. Only leave something in your room with a long string hanging from it out the window, so that I can pull it and make a noise when I need you."

They settled on Norah's comb, which was aluminum and would fall to the floor lightly enough not to disturb the rest of the household, but would make enough noise to rouse Norah.

"Not that I'm likely to be sleepin', I'll be that worried about you. Be careful, won't you?"

Hilda took off her cap and apron and put on a black hat and a cloak that would conceal as well as warm. With the sun down the evening would be chilly. As soon as the house was quiet she crept, boots in hand, down the back stairs with Norah. After she put her boots back on, Hilda took the time to steal down to the basement storeroom for a lantern and to get some matches from the kitchen, and then she was ready. The two girls hugged, Norah repeated her injunction to be careful, and Hilda stepped out into the night.

Her first problem was the dog Rex. He liked Hilda and wanted to go with her, saying so in eager little whines that threatened to become barks.

"Be quiet, Rex, that is a good dog! You cannot come with me. *Be quiet!*" He subsided at last with one disappointed whine.

The wind was rising. Hilda pulled the cloak more tightly to

herself and hurried. She had a good deal of territory to cover in the time left to her. She decided to go first to the police station, just to make sure Viktor was safely imprisoned. Then she would wake Ingrid Lindahl and make her tell where the spare key to the Warren house was kept, and then meet the men there to surprise a murderer and a thief. There was enough time, but barely. She stepped up her pace.

The police station, when she got there, was dark. She wasn't quite sure why that surprised her. Like firemen, policemen on night duty slept until they were called out. But with a prisoner in the jail, an important prisoner? She had expected more signs of activity.

Furthermore, it made her job harder. She had intended to walk in, determine that Viktor was being looked after properly, and leave. Now how was she to rouse anyone, without making a great fuss she didn't want?

Maybe there was an easier way. She knew where the four jail cells were. Everyone knew that, since they had bars on the windows. The windows were high, but there were those ash barrels in the alley . . .

Her progress was slow and somewhat noisy. She had to roll one of the barrels under the first window, light her lantern—no easy matter with the gusty wind—and then climb up on the barrel, lantern in hand. When she had finally accomplished it, she was barely tall enough to see into the cell, but what she saw was discouraging. All four cots were empty.

So it was all to do over again, maybe several times, and she was growing nervous. This was taking time, time she could ill afford. She checked the second cell, the third, with no result. In an agony of impatience she shoved one last time at the heavy barrel. It tipped over.

She instantly put out the lantern and flattened herself against the wall, not daring to breathe. Surely they would hear!

But there was no outcry, no light. When her heart stopped pounding, she realized there had been no sound from the last cell, either. How could Viktor have failed to hear that hollow thud as the barrel fell right under his window? Unless—unless they had mistreated him, and he was—was ill, or worse!

She pulled the barrel upright, climbed on it with scant ceremony, and lit the lantern again, shining it down into the last cell.
Empty.

She jumped down, catching her hem on a barrel stave. She
heard the stitches give, but she couldn't take the time to worry
about it. Now she had to find Viktor!

He had not done as he was told. He had been too afraid.
Now, she very much feared, he was still at the Avery house, and
that might ruin her plans! She would have to go and get him out
and take him with her. Still more time wasted.

She darkened her lantern, tucked her trailing skirt up, and
made off at a run.

The Avery house was dark, as were its neighbors. Well, that
was to be expected at—what—nearly midnight? It would be
locked, too. Hilda was not, at this point, prepared to let that stop
her. She had climbed in windows before, and surely the kitchen
window, at least, would be open.

It was. She was up and inside in less than a minute, and was
feeling her way down the hall to the back stairs when she heard
footsteps.

Someone was on the stairs!

Probably it was Viktor, having gotten up the courage to leave
at last. But suppose it was the cook? Did the cook live in? Or the
butler. Was there one?

Hilda's feet moved more quickly than her thoughts. Without
quite knowing how she got there, she was through the hall door
and into her old hiding place under the stairs, with the door
pulled nearly shut.

It was an excellent place for concealment. It was not, however, a good place to hear anything that went on beyond the
heavy door to the service wing. Strain though she might, she
could hear nothing. She was nearly ready to leave her sanctuary
when she did hear something, and the sound froze her blood.

Softly, quietly, someone was descending the stairs over her
head.

There was a stumble at the foot of the stairs, a muffled

outcry, a thud as something—someone?—fell heavily against the table that stood next to the stairs.

The table moved under the weight and pushed against the cupboard door. Pushed just enough.

Hilda heard the *snick* as the latch caught.

She was a prisoner.

Even with the door tightly shut, she could hear faint sounds from the front of the house. She thought she heard the entryway door open and close, and then a soft sound that might have been the front door closing. Then nothing more.

She was hot in her woolen cloak, she was nearly suffocating from the smell of camphor, and she was furious with herself. What a stupid predicament! And how was she to get herself out?

She dared not make an outcry. She dared not light the lantern. Who knew what flammable goods might be stored in the tiny cubbyhole? She would be burned alive if she started a fire in her prison.

Frantically she poked around for anything that might spring the latch. Her groping fingers encountered only soft cloth, the leather of boots and shoes, a few unidentifiable lumps. She had stirred up the camphor flakes; she nearly choked.

The temperature was growing unbearable. She threw off her cloak; it tangled in her hat and she nearly cried with frustration. She did cry as she stuck her finger on her hat pin in trying to free the heavy folds of wool.

Then the cry changed to a low, steady series of wholly regrettable words in Swedish as she cursed herself for a fool. It took only a moment to pull out the hat pin, work it into the latch, and push back the catch. She was free.

There was no time now to worry about quiet and caution. She took a few grateful deep breaths and then headed for the back stairs and the attic. One look around, as the moon came out from behind ragged clouds for a moment, told her that Viktor had gone. Probably it *had* been his footsteps on the back stairs, and she need not have wasted so much time.

She was late! And all might yet be lost! She grasped her lantern firmly, pinned her hat back on her head with a vicious jab, and left the house at a dead run.

She was still a few doors from the Warren house, in the next block, when she knew she was too late. Something was happening there. She could hear shouts, cries, the sounds of a struggle. Lights were beginning to show in neighbors' windows as the gas was turned up.

She panted to a stop and lit her own lantern. She saw, emerging from the side of the house, two groups of men. Flynn Murphy and John Bolton had firm hold of Viktor Kovacz. And in the hands of two men she did not know, Herbert Avery struggled furiously, shouting above the wind.

"Let me *go*, you ruffians! He's the man you want! He's a thief—a thief and a murderer!"

26

ENGLAND FAVORS LYNCH LAW
—headline in South Bend *Tribune,* September 17, 1901

THE neighbors were beginning to come out of their houses now. Frightened women in their wrappers peered out of windows while their menfolk, in hastily donned trousers, came out to see what the uproar was about. A few carried lanterns. One, Hilda was appalled to see, held a large and terrifying revolver.

Avery had an audience now. He raised his voice further. "Gentlemen, I appeal to you! This man has broken into Mrs. Warren's house. I have no doubt he is her murderer, come back to steal money from the woman he killed!"

Cries of "Shame!" rose up. Encouraged, Avery went on. "I was trying to apprehend the miscreant when these men set upon me. Whether they are in league with the criminal, or—"

"Hey, they caught him, too, didn't they?" roared one voice, but the rest were caught up in the rhetoric. The crowd was swelling. Avery went on shouting, passionately.

Hilda could see but one way out. While the attention was on Avery, she wrapped her black cloak around her for invisibility and made her way over to Viktor, still held by Flynn and John.

"Move him away a little, out of the light," she said to the captors, her voice taut with urgency. "And then when no one is looking, Viktor, run—run as fast as you can to the police!"

He was white with panic; his eyes darted to the crowd.

"Viktor, you did not do as I said before, and now you are in terrible trouble. Do as I say now, if you value your life!"

John looked at Hilda. She gritted her teeth. "John, make him do it. I know what I do!"

He came to a decision and nodded grimly. "I brought one of the horses, just in case. We'll get him away." He and Flynn began slowly, gradually, to ease Viktor away.

Avery was stirring the crowd to action. Kapinski and So-bieski (Hilda assumed) still held him in a tight grip, but public opinion was against them. Hilda, praying for time, found the broken window at the back of the Warren house and climbed in. There was a telephone, she was sure—if she could find it—if it was still working—if she could rouse the operator—ah, there it was! She picked up the mouthpiece and turned the crank.

After an agonizing interval a sleepy voice answered. "Number, please?"

"I must speak with the police, please, and hurry!"

A further interval. Another sleepy voice, male this time. "Central police station."

"God be thanked! A man is coming to you, a man named Viktor Kovacz. There are—who is this speaking, please?"

"Patrolman Lefkowicz."

Hilda would have fallen on her knees if there had been time. "Mr. Lefkowicz, I am Hilda Johansson. Please do not think I am crazy. Mr. Kovacz will come to you, soon, and you must put him in the jail. He has done nothing, but there are men after him, and—"

There was a great roar outside the house. Hilda dropped the mouthpiece and ran to the front door. The men were running now, their lanterns swaying wildly. Hilda could hear the cries. "After him! He's getting away!"

There was one more thing she could do. Though the idea terrified her, she went back to the telephone and spoke into it. "Mr. Lefkowicz? Are you still there?"

He was not. She spared a very quick moment for a prayer that he had understood and would do as she asked, and then de-pressed the switch and turned the crank again.

The operator was awake now. "I wish, please, to speak to Mr. Oliver. Mr. James Oliver."

The crowd, by the time it reached Main Street, was large, angry, and diverse. The well-to-do neighbors of the Warrens and Averys mingled with the small businessmen who lived above their shops and the workers in boardinghouses closer to the center of town. Some had made torches, fierce flares that wavered in the wind and cast ominous shadows. Not everyone knew whom they were chasing, or why, but they knew that something, at last, was happening, something that gathered the tensions of the past weeks and brought them to a head. They ran for the sake of action, shouted for the sake of primitive instinct. The crowd had become a mob.

It converged on the police station and on the law, embodied in the person of Patrolman Lefkowicz, who stood, white and strained but courageous, to face it.

The mob had adopted Avery as its spokesman. He had long since freed himself from his captors. Now he stepped forward to challenge Lefkowicz.

"There's a murderer running loose! What do you propose to do about it?"

Angry shouts and murmurs.

Lefkowicz held up his hand. "If you mean Mr. Kovacz, he is in jail and will remain there."

The murmurs diminished. For some, Kovacz's capture was enough.

"Oh, will he?" Avery continued. "Or will you let him go as you did the other one? Are we never to be safe in our beds? Must more innocent men and women be killed?"

This was rhetoric the mob could taste, as they could already taste blood. They began to close in.

Lefkowicz held up his hand again. In his other, a revolver appeared. "The police will take care of this. One of the dead men was my own cousin. Do you not think I will do everything that is to be done?"

Something in his accent caught the attention of a few of the angry men. One of them shouted, "Another dirty foreigner, ain't you? Protecting your own, never mind about decent Americans!"

More shouts, more movement. Torches flared. The crowd surged. Lefkowicz raised his gun to fire into the air.

An open landau charged around the corner, drawn by two horses, hooves clattering. The mob moved away in confusion. The landau came to a stop directly in front of the police station.

It held a man and, surprisingly, a woman. As the mob muttered, unsure of what to do about this new development, the man stood, and climbed to the carriage seat.

He was not a tall man, but from his position atop the seat he towered over the crowd. A few of the men recognized him, then a few more. The mutterings grew quieter.

"Well, now," said James Oliver, "it's a little late for a party, isn't it, gentlemen?"

A nervous titter or two, then silence.

"I'm surprised to see you here, Avery," he went on conversationally. "Thought you had better sense."

Avery made no reply.

"Understand you've accused someone of stealing."

Avery got his voice back. "Yes, and I can prove it. I caught him in the act!"

More murmurs. Oliver reached out a hand; the coachman put the buggy whip into it. Oliver scowled at Avery and put out his lower lip. "I see. And while we're on the subject of stealing, what is my marble doing in your front hall?"

He snapped the whip. The woman on the seat whispered something to him. "And what did you hope to gain by killing Mrs. Warren? That's the act of a coward and a blackguard, Avery!"

He snapped the whip again.

Avery turned and looked at the crowd. They were silent now, their faces intent as they listened to Oliver. "Answer him, why don't you?" someone shouted.

Avery's nerve broke at last. He bolted. Straight through the center of the crowd he ran, surprising them so much they let him go. Their confusion was only for a moment; then they would have gone after him, but Oliver snapped his whip again, and Lefkowicz fired his revolver.

"Let him go!" commanded the second-most-important man in town. His was a voice accustomed to public speaking, and accustomed to command; the mob hesitated.

"He has no place to run. Let the police deal with him now. He is thrice a murderer and unnamed times a thief. Leave him to the law!"

Perhaps Avery heard him. The crowd watched as he ran down a narrow alley, stopped and turned, and then ran on.

Only the one or two who followed saw him cross Michigan Street and continue down that dark alley. One of them, realizing where the alley ended, shouted at him to stop, but he did not stop.

Over the rising wind, none of the mob, more than a block away, heard the splash as the cold, black waters of the St. Joseph River closed over Herbert Avery.

27

The love of money is the root of all evil.
—The First Epistle of Paul the Apostle to Timothy

ow did you know? And why didn't you ask me for help?"
It was Wednesday afternoon. Hilda, yawning frequently,
was sitting with Patrick in Howard Park. The day was
chilly, but sunny, and she was warm enough in a shawl. She had
already explained everything in snatches to the other servants;
now it was Patrick's turn.

She answered the second question first. It was the important
one, after all. Patrick was jealous, and though that was somewhat
gratifying, it was also troubling. She did not, for reasons she preferred not to analyze, want him to stay angry with her.

"There was not time, Patrick, I thought that Mr. Avery
would try to steal the money as soon as he could, and without
that as proof of his wickedness, I had nothing. I knew no one
would believe me, that a man so important could steal and kill.
And John, I could tell him easily, and he could get the others.
Also I did not care—not so much—if they were to be in danger."

The last wasn't strictly true, but Hilda thought Patrick
would like to hear it. He did, too. His sulky look changed to a
self-satisfied one.

"So how did you know it was Avery? It looked like Kovacz."

She nodded vigorously while quickly sorting out what to tell
Patrick. She had no intention of revealing Viktor's terrible bargain. Since it had never been carried out, it was between him
and his conscience.

"I knew Viktor had put the flag over the body. Or I thought he had; his hair oil was on it. But I could not understand why he would kill the man who paid his wages. It would be—there is a saying—'cutting your face—' " She stopped, perplexed.

" 'Cutting your nose off to spite your face'?"

"Yes, that is it! It was foolish, and I did not think Viktor was a fool. Though he did foolish things, he and John and Flynn and the rest!" she added with a self-righteous sniff.

"So what put you onto Avery?"

"I should have known before I did. I was very slow and stupid. I knew that Mr. Warren did not want to sell that property to Mr. Avery. I heard him say so, when they were at a dinner party here one night. And he was very angry about it. And yet, when he was dead, Mr. Avery bought the land and gave Mrs. Warren the money for it."

"I don't understand what that had to do with—"

"Wait, and I will tell you. I did not think anything about that. But I learned three things when I went to the Averys' and had to hide in the cupboard—the first time I went." She avoided catching Patrick's eye. She knew how he felt about some of her more outrageous activities. "I learned that though Mr. Avery might flirt with other ladies, he really was—very fond of Mrs. Avery." Her cheeks colored as she remembered how she knew. She hastened on.

"I thought then that he might wish to give her anything she wanted. And she wanted that land. I do not know why, to be certain—"

"I heard something," Patrick interrupted, "just a few days ago. I didn't connect it with this, but just maybe . . . where was the land Avery bought, anyway?"

"I do not know."

"Well, if it was south of town, they both had good reason to want it. They're going to extend the electric railway line out there one of these days, and land'll be goin' like hotcakes! He stood to make a good deal of money on it, seems to me. And to cheat Warren out of a good deal."

Hilda considered that. "She was a woman who liked money,

I think." She talked about Mrs. Avery as though she had died. Perhaps, so far as society was concerned, she had.

"You said three things," Patrick prodded.

"Yes. I learned that there was new green marble in the entryway of the Warren house."

Patrick nodded. "Stolen from the city hall building site."

"I did not know that, of course, not to be certain, but I was interested. And then when Mr. Warren talked about the blue jar standing in the sun—"

"What blue jar? What are you talkin' about? Here, is that sun too hot on you?"

"Patrick! I do not get crazy! When I went to Mrs. Warren's house, after she had died, I looked through the front door and saw in the hallway a big blue jar, for umbrellas and sticks, I think. It was very bright in the sun."

She waited. Patrick shook his head, still frowning.

"Patrick! Think! When I was at that house before, it was a house of mourning. The shades were down. There was no sun inside. And the sticks were in a brass umbrella stand. Ingrid told me herself that Mrs. Warren had made her bring the blue jar down from the attic, only that morning, the morning the poor lady died. She wished to take the good brass one with her, I think, and thought she could leave the ugly blue one, the one she did not like, behind for the new owners."

Patrick thought about that. "So Avery was in the house that morning."

"Yes! And he lied about it to his wife. He said the last time he saw Mrs. Warren was the day I was there, the day he gave her the money for the land."

"It wasn't much to go on."

"No, and I still was not certain. I could not believe that a man would kill only to buy land. But when I went to Mr. Oliver, he told me that he had offered Mr. Warren a bonus if the city hall was finished on time. And Mr. Warren needed money; that I could see myself, from the state of his house.

"I knew then that Mr. Avery had done the bad things at the city hall. He wished to cost Mr. Warren money so that he would sell him the land to get money. I think Mr. Avery went that night to steal some more, when he heard that the night watchman was not there. He did not think anyone would be there. When Mr. Warren caught him . . ."

"Hmmm. Well, it hangs together. But it was all speculation, mind!"

"That is why we had to set a trap for him. And it would have worked much better if Viktor had done as he was told!" Hilda was still wroth about her orders being disobeyed.

"Now, see, I don't understand that, either. How was Kovacz mixed up in this whole thing? What was he doin' at the city hall that night, with the flag and all? What was he doin' goin' to see Mrs. Warren?"

"He went to visit her to get his money," Hilda said carefully, answering Patrick's last question and hoping he would forget the others. "She had asked him to do a job for her, and had not yet paid him. But she was not a very nice lady, I think. She would not pay him, and he quarreled with her. That is why he ran away when he learned she was dead. He was afraid Ingrid had heard them."

"I suppose that's why he went back that night, too—to get his money?"

"I think so, yes. Nearly he ruined everything! If it had not been for Mr. Oliver—"

"I wonder you had the nerve to go and wake him up. He could've made mincemeat of you, me girl!"

"I was afraid, but not so afraid as I would have been a few days ago. I had talked to him, Patrick, and he is not a bad man. A little—strict—"

Patrick snorted. "A little! He's a Scots Presbyterian, that's what he is! You're lucky you're still in one piece!"

"Viktor, he is the lucky one, I think. Those people, Patrick, the mob . . ." She shuddered.

Patrick shook his head sadly. "It wouldn't've been the first time an innocent man'd been lynched."

Hilda didn't want to comment on the subject of Viktor's innocence, or lack of it. She gave her attention to her hair, straightened her hat. "There is one thing, though, that I still do not understand, Patrick. Still I do not know what is planned at Studebaker's, and I worry."

Patrick's dimples showed. His blue eyes twinkled. He smoothed his mustache with two elegant swipes of a hand. "As it happens, I know that, meself."

"Patrick! Tell me!"

He told her.

"*That* is all it is?"

"*All?* I'll have you know, me girl, it's the most important thing that's happened in this town in its whole history! It'll change South Bend forever, that's what it'll do!"

"Yes, but—oh, Patrick, and I was so worried!" She began to laugh. The laugh changed to an uncontrollable giggle. It was infectious. Patrick laughed. The people near them in the park laughed in sympathy.

A few yards beyond them, the mighty river flowed past, impassive, inexorable, eternal.

Afterword

On September 19, 1901, the memorial service for President McKinley was held in the Auditorium. The entire Studebaker family attended. Colonel George was a member of the organizing committee. His wife played the organ for the choral music. Mrs. Herbert Avery did not attend.

On September 28, 1901, the South Bend *Tribune* published a story verifying the visit of Leon Czolgosz, alias Fred Nieman, "a few weeks before his attack upon the president."

On November 16, 1901, Studebaker Brothers Manufacturing Company unveiled its first automobile, a light truck powered by electricity, in a trial run down the streets of South Bend.

On November 27, 1901, after a decline lasting several weeks, Mr. Clement Studebaker died peacefully at his home.